The Long Way Home

The Long Way Home

JERRY JERMAN

VICTOR BOOKS

A DIVISION OF SCRIPTURE PRESS PUBLICATIONS INC.
USA CANADA ENGLAND

THE JOURNEYS OF JESSIE LAND

The Long Way Home
My Father the Horse Thief
Phantom of the Pueblo (July, 1995)
Danger at Outlaw Creek (July, 1995)

Cover design by Scott Rattray
Cover illustration by Michael Garland
Copyediting by Afton Rorvik, Liz Duckworth

Library of Congress Cataloging-in-Publication Data

Jerman, Jerry.
    The long way home / by Jerry Jerman.
      p.   c. — (The Journeys of Jessie Land)
    Summary: Desperate to escape an overbearing aunt and find her parents in California, twelve-year-old Jessie stows away in the truck of two men traveling across the dust-plagued West in 1935, relying on her faith in times of trouble.
    ISBN 1-56476-272-6
    [1. Voyages and travels—Fiction. 2. Depressions—1929—Fiction. 3. Christian life—Fiction.] I. Title. II. Series: Jerman, Jerry, 1949–   Journeys of Jessie Land.
PZ7.J54Lo   1994
[Fic]—dc20   94-33939
                                           CIP
                                           AC

1 2 3 4 5 6 7 8 9 10 Printing/Year 99 98 97 96 95

499

*To Charlene, Emily, Hadley, and Andrew
with all my love.*

*I wish to thank
the Society of Children's Book
Writers and Illustrators
for a Work in Progress grant
which enabled me to complete this book.*

Chapter 1

I was trapped!

Clutching Mama's letter in my hand, fighting back tears, I gazed out the dusty curtains on the front door. Through the raging dust storm, I could just make out the faded red gasoline pump and the large, scratched sign. *Gasoline and Good Food.*

It was May 4, 1935. It seemed like the dust had been blowing my whole life.

Behind me my nine-year-old cousin Walter Tyler stuck his pug nose up at me and sneered, "Jessie Land, your folks ain't never gonna send for you. You're probably gonna live here with us for good."

My backside still smarting from my last spanking, I stood with this little, blond-headed rascal in the hallway of his parents' house that Saturday afternoon in Liberal, Kansas. I was three years older and I wanted to poke that boy. Poke him hard. But I was raised different. Besides, Aunt Edna had just whacked me good after I tried to pull up Walter's dust mask. And I'd only been trying to help the boy!

I tugged down my dust mask—a faded bandanna—so

he could see my mouth. Then I told him, "Walter Scott"—he hated to be called Walter Scott—"you don't know what you're talking about. I got a letter just this morning from Mama and Daddy."

Walter's lower lip sprouted out. His pale nose and cheeks were dotted with freckles. "Phoo. I know what it says."

An anger rose up in me. Aunt Edna always opened my letters from Mama and Daddy, no doubt searching for money. I had once asked her not to open my mail, but she regarded this as sassing her and had spanked me good.

"Besides," Walter said, "I know the *real* reason they left you behind."

I felt my face flush. Maybe he did know, but I didn't want to think about that. Instead, I unfolded the letter and studied it again. It was dated April 26.

Dear Jessie,

We miss you like the dickens. We have found Work at the McCallister farm, near San Bernardino. The owners, who seem nice enough, tell us there will be enough Work for us till May 9. They'll let us stay on here till noon of May 10. Then we'll be moving on again.

Jobs are very scarce out here and we must keep going where the Harvests are. Honey, I know we promised to send for you after six months, but we just don't have the money saved up yet. Our Hope is to have enough money in six more months so we can

finally send for you. In the meantime I Pray God will
send you a Guardian Angel to watch over you.
Love, Mama

*Oh, Mama, how could you and Daddy leave me? And
why?* But I knew why and tears welled up in my eyes
again. *How can I forgive you for leaving me behind?*

I stared hard at Walter and argued back, "The real
reason they left me behind is they didn't need to be
traipsing out to California with a kid."

Maybe it wasn't the real reason, but it made good
sense. Still, it hurt. The fact was they left me behind
here, in the care of Mama's sister.

Walter just smirked and tugged at the dirty red bandanna around his neck. I put my dust mask back on. With a
day like this it made sense to keep it on, even indoors.
There were enough troubles in life without getting dust
pneumonia. I'd already seen it in one of Walter's little
sisters, Ruth Ann. Her eyes and nose got as red as the
bandanna she wouldn't use. Then she coughed up nasty
gobs of mud. Fortunately, an early visit to the doctor
brought her around again.

Someone rattled up to the gas pump outside. A horn
blew four times.

I looked for Walter, but he had disappeared. And he
was in charge of the pumps that afternoon.

Pulling my dust mask snug, I went out the squeaky
front door. The day looked like all the others—brown
haze in the sky, sand and grit blowing across the road

from the dead field the Dillons used to farm. I imagined
the Arab lands looking like this. And feeling like it too.
My eyes stung. There'd been no rain for a long time and
the wind seemed bent on blowing the whole country
away. Mama said it was in the good Lord's hands. He'd
change it when He saw fit.

The horn blasted again. I hustled over to the old, black
Ford pickup truck parked beside the pump.

Two men sat in the cab with the windows rolled up.
What I took to be all their earthly possessions lay heaped
in back under a heavy, green canvas. The pickup looked
like a hundred other vehicles I'd seen on this road, head-
ing west toward California. Like Mama and Daddy.

A plump man with stringy, brown hair sat hunched
over the wheel. His black eyes glowed behind a pair of
bent spectacles. The other man I couldn't make out too
well, what with all the grit and scratches on the glass.

"How much gas do you want?" I called out.

I figured the driver would roll down the window or
open the door. Instead, he tapped three quarters on the
glass.

What nerve! People ought to be courteous enough to
speak to you directly.

I opened the gas cap. Then I grasped the rough, wood-
en handle of the old gas pump and worked it until the
gasoline surged into the glass globe. Once enough gas
filled the globe, I stopped pumping. With both hands I
struggled to get the nozzle into the gas tank.

A door opened and slammed shut.

"You need a hand there, missy?" someone asked.

Through the flying dust I glimpsed one of the most remarkable men I'd ever seen.

He was the other man from the pickup. Tall and straight, he was much older than the driver, his hair gray and his skin pale and wrinkled. His long, white moustache stretched downward around the corners of his mouth. A splash of white beard clung to his chin. He tugged his black cowboy hat down against the storm. He was dressed in black pants and jacket and a faded purple shirt with a pair of polished green boots. I liked those polished boots. Daddy would've like them too. We both admired those who maintained their possessions.

He grabbed the nozzle from my hands and plunged it easily into the gas tank.

"Thank you, sir, but I think I could've managed," I told him.

"I just hate to see a girl do a man's work is all," he explained. He pumped gasoline into the tank.

"I'm as fully fit for this work as any man."

His head jerked toward me, his thick, gray eyebrows arched up.

"You speak right up, don't you?"

"I never saw any reason to shy away from folks," I confessed.

Despite the dust swirling around us, he smiled. It was a genuine smile. I liked him.

I pointed at the green canvas covering the things in the truck bed. "Are you headed for California?"

The man nodded. He shielded his eyes and watched the gas drain from the glass globe of the pump.

"My mama and daddy are there now," I told him. "I just got a letter from them. They're near San Bernardino."

"San Bernardino you say?" He yanked out the nozzle. "Well, what're you doing here?"

What could I tell him? The truth?

"I'm staying here until Mama and Daddy get settled."

"I see," he said, his eyes firm on me like he was sizing me up. "We're going through San Bernardino ourselves. In a matter of days. On our way to Harvest-of-Gold, California." He hung up the nozzle.

My heart raced. *These men will be passing through San Bernardino, the very place where Mama and Daddy are right now. The very place!*

"Excuse me, missy," the man said, stepping around me. I moved, but I kept thinking about Mama and Daddy. He pounded on the Ford's door something fierce. "Awright, Lavern, let's settle up."

The driver cracked open the door. The smell of sweat exploded from inside the car. Lavern held out the quarters.

"We need some food," he grunted. He dropped more change into the older man's hand. "And, Tom, put some water in the blasted radiator. It's heating up already today."

He slammed his door shut.

Tom muttered under his breath. When he turned to me, though, he smiled again. I admired adults who knew when to curb their tongues and put on a pleasant face.

"Think you could drum up something for us to eat?" he asked. He laid the quarters in the palm of my outstretched hand, then he held out four dimes. "Maybe a couple of sandwiches, two slices of pie, and a jar of coffee?"

I nodded and closed my hand over the coins. Before I ran back into the house, I looked back and saw him wrestling with the water hose.

Walter pounced on me the minute I stepped inside. He knocked me against the wall, peeling the coins from my fist.

"Gimme that money," he demanded. "It's not yours."

"Give me a chance to hand it over," I snapped.

He struck my arm with his fist. The little brute! I'd taken enough from him today. I shoved him away. He howled, dropping the coins onto the floor.

"Mama!" he cried out. "Jessie hit me!" He ran off.

What a mama's boy. I knew I'd be in for it. His mama was partial to him, for what reason I didn't know. He bore the spitting image of his father. Uncle Rudy lay in his bedroom, weak with some mysterious illness. Or so Aunt Edna told Mama. But just last week, with my aunt gone to town, I saw Uncle Rudy spring right out of bed. He danced over to the bureau and fetched a bottle and drank it half down. Whiskey! The only mysterious part of this illness was how he fooled Aunt Edna.

I picked up the quarters and dimes and dropped them into the cigar box in the hall. Then I went into the kitchen for the food.

My aunt was drying Walter's ridiculous tears with a corner of her apron. Walter himself kept shuddering as if a great offense had been committed against him.

Of course my aunt took Walter's side. She turned on me. "Jessica Whitney Land, why on earth did you hit Walter?" she demanded.

Hit! I had learned certain things living among these Tylers. One was that anything out of Walter's mouth became gospel. But I'd been taught to tell the truth, regardless of how it might be received.

"I pushed him away because he treated me like a thief and hit me in the hall," I told her.

"That's not what Walter said."

I glared at my cousin.

Aunt Edna grabbed me by the hair and hauled me over to a family picture on the wall.

"Why can't you be like these children?" she snapped. "You don't see any of them causing trouble and getting spanked every single day."

I winced in pain. All I saw were my aunt's disobedient children. Then the glass on the picture threw my reflection back at me. What I saw was my mama's brown eyes and a determined chin with a dimple in it just like Daddy's. I saw my red hair, clipped short as a boy's, and remembered my aunt first taking the scissors to me six months ago. "I'll not waste my time fussing with your hair," she'd said as my lovely curly locks fell to the floor. Mama had loved my hair so.

I saw something else in the glass and shuddered. My

aunt had reached over to the counter and fetched a large wooden spoon. Her arm flew up as she forced me to bend over.

Smack! Smack! Smack! Smack! Smack!

Five painful and humiliating blows delivered to my rear! It hurt like the devil. I couldn't look at her or at Walter. This was *true* injustice!

Aunt Edna declared, "Young lady, your misbehavior wears on a body. You go back to the bedroom and sit a spell and think about what you've done. When you're ready to apologize to Walter, you come back and do so."

Apologize! I'd never apologize. Or forgive him either. Or her. *Never!* Not ever!

I swallowed my pride, tears, and everything else. They tasted vile. Then I sniffed and said, "Those men out there paid forty cents for sandwiches, pie, and a jar of coffee."

"I'll attend to it. You just do as you're told."

I rushed away just as the first tears burst from my eyes. I wouldn't let them see me cry. *Never!*

Chapter 2

Back in the bedroom Walter's three younger brothers were poking a stick at a bug that had made the sorry mistake of sticking its head through a crack in the floor. When the bug decided to make a break for it, they yelled and chased it out of the room.

I went over to one of the beds and dropped onto it. My backside hurt but not near as much as my heart. I took my tattered Bible from the bedside table and opened it to the back. On one of the blank end pages I had printed the letters *AE* for Aunt Edna. In rows under the letters were at least a hundred short, black marks. One for every spanking, haircut, and harsh word Aunt Edna'd given me. I took out my pencil and scratched another. Every mark brought back the pain and the shame. Three teardrops splattered across the page. I blotted them with my hand.

On the opposite page were the letters *M&D* for Mama and Daddy. I'd only made two marks on that page—one for leaving me behind and one that morning for not sending for me after six months.

"Mama, Daddy," I pleaded to the empty room, "why can't I be with you?"

I looked through the window at the sand and dirt blowing in the reddish-brown air. I could make out the black
shape of the Ford pickup from where I sat. I caught myself thinking, *If only those men would take me with them.
They're headed for California. I could be with Mama and
Daddy before they leave that farm!*

My parents had always taught me to go to my knees in
troubled times. I slipped to the floor, clasped my hands,
and prayed, "Dear Lord, I'm truly miserable. I can't believe You wish a family to be apart so. Please help me,
Lord. Please—"

The Ford's horn blasted into the room, spoiling my talk
with God. I looked up, annoyed.

I went back to my prayer. Where was I?

Ooooeeeeeegaaa! The horn again.

I jumped up, furious at that spiteful man behind the
wheel. Why didn't he just. . . .

A crazy, crazy, crazy thought popped into my head. *I
could go with those men, couldn't I? Lots of folks were headed west. Why not me?*

"Walter!" Aunt Edna cried from the kitchen. The sandwiches were ready. The men would be leaving. I had to
decide what to do. And decide now!

Suddenly determined, I said to myself, "I'll do it! I'll
go!"

Acting fast, I grabbed a clean pillowcase from the dress-
er. I had $3 hid in my Bible. The money had been safe
since none of those little Tylers ever went near God's
Word. I laid the Bible in the pillowcase and threw in an

extra pair of underwear and socks, a clean shirt, and my
magazine pictures. I grabbed my doll Marjorie and stuffed
her inside too.

I crept out of the room and back down the hall. At the
door to the kitchen, I spied Aunt Edna pouring coffee into
a jar. The bug-torturing boys had cornered the poor creature under the oven. The rest of the Tyler kids I heard in
the other bedroom with Uncle Rudy. Walter was nowhere
to be seen.

I slipped down the hall, stepping over the floorboards I
knew would groan. Instead of going out the squealing
front door, I decided to use a side one my aunt was less
likely to hear. I tugged out the oily rags stuffed in the
crack to keep out the dirt. Opening the door, I stepped
out into the dry, dusty air. The terrible blow hurt my
eyes. I pulled up my dust mask and set out for the Ford.

But when I started around the corner, I stopped short.
Walter! The little scamp hadn't come when his mother
called. He sat outside the front door on a wooden crate.
His bandanna hung around his neck even though he was
outdoors in a dust storm! I almost pitied him. The boy
lacked sense.

Pitiful or not, he blocked my way. I couldn't run out to
that pickup and let him see me. The little tattletale would
surely spoil my escape.

I hid at the side of the house, waiting. Then a big
question hit me. Should I just go up to the men and ask
for a ride outright or should I sneak in back of the pickup
without asking permission? The man Tom might be will-

ing to help me. About the other man I couldn't be sure. Probably he wouldn't see a child with three dollars as an opportunity. Still, I didn't like the idea of being a stow-away. Until today, I'd never been a sneak.

"Walter!" my aunt called out again.

I waited for the longest time until I heard the front door slam. Then I peeked around the corner.

Walter was gone. My chance!

Clutching my bundle, I hurried past the front of the house. The blow had picked up, turning the world a swirling reddish-brown. I pressed my mask tightly against my nose. The awful grit rained in my eyes, but for the first time ever I was thankful for a dust storm. Nobody in the house or the Ford would be able to see me.

As I neared the pickup, doubts hammered at me. *What if the men wouldn't give me a ride? If they refused me, how would I make my way west?* I only knew Mama and Daddy's whereabouts for six more days, until noon of May 10 when they'd have to leave that farm.

I heard the front door of the house slam.

Walter! I was about to be caught!

Wrong as it might be, I decided to stow away. I raced to the back of the Ford and stepped up on the bumper. Two wooden chairs stacked together made a kind of opening, like the mouth to a cave. Next to the chairs the canvas sagged a little where the rope hung loose. I might be able to work myself into that gap. Before I climbed over the tailgate, though, I glanced at the cab.

The old man, Tom, had turned around. He stared

plumb at me.

I had been found out!

* * *

I huddled scared in the back of that pickup. The old man, Tom, had seen me all right. Looked me eye-to-eye. I just knew he'd turn to that stringy-haired man behind the wheel, that Lavern, and say, "We got us a girl stowaway." Then Lavern would stomp around to the back and haul me out.

But it never happened. After Walter brought the men their food, the pickup fired, and we set out with a jerk.

Was I really on my way? Headed for California? Would I really be reunited with Mama and Daddy after six long, terrible months?

Twisting in the narrow space beneath the hot, sour-smelling canvas, I tried to get comfortable. Something jabbed my side. Running my hands over the shapes, I made out tools—a pickax, shovel, hatchet, and hammer. They lay heaped beside me. On the other side a large cardboard box pressed against me. I tried to scoot it over but it wouldn't budge.

My hand fell on another piece of metal. What was it? A pipe? Then my fingers discovered a hammer and a grip and a trigger.

A gun! Dear Lord, what kind of men are these? Criminals? Then, thinking it over, I realized that even Uncle Rudy had a couple of guns locked up in a case in his house. I shoved the weapon away and tried not to think about it.

For a while I lay awake thinking about how I was finally free of Aunt Edna. *Free!* I'd never have to make any more marks in my Bible. Even if I had to ride all the way to California under this stifling canvas, it was worth it. I stretched out as much as possible. I took my doll Marjorie from my bundle, rested my head on the pillowcase, and closed my eyes. I figured it still to be early afternoon, but the pickup's rocking motion made me drowsy. I guess I slipped off to sleep.

I don't recall any dreams, except for Mama's voice calling my name. "Jessie, Jessie." Like I was outside and she was calling me in to supper.

I woke with a jerk.

The pickup lurched, swerved over to the side of the road, and skidded to a stop. The pickax slid hard into me. I used all my strength to keep it from squashing me against the cardboard box.

I heard the pickup door open, then the tramp of feet.

Then, unexpectedly, the canvas flew off.

I jumped as a muddy-brown sky spread over me. In the middle of this sky burst Lavern's face. He leaned into the truck bed. I sat up fast, my heart beating like crazy. The smell of his sweat filled my head. Light glinted off his bent spectacles.

"Awright, you," he growled. "You get yourself out of there right now!"

Chapter 3

I'd never seen anything grimier than this man's round face. Patches of dirt clung to his sweaty cheeks and chin. His thin hair lay plastered to his head. Behind ratty eyeglasses his black eyes flashed, like the eyes of a terrifying creature.

"I told you, girlie, to get yourself *out!*" he hollered, shaking his head.

I gasped and tried to edge away from him. Taking a quick look around, I saw nothing but a dusty, empty plain with a road stuck in the middle of it.

"Get out, get out!" Lavern shrieked, flapping his arms.

I picked up my bundle and Marjorie and started to climb out. My back and neck ached after riding all those miles. My legs felt stiff. I didn't move fast enough to suit Lavern. He grabbed my arm and yanked me to the ground.

My anger burned up my fear of the man. *"Ow!* You nearly broke my arm."

"Leave that youngster alone," Tom ordered.

"You're on her side!" Lavern blubbered. "You saw her sneak on and you didn't even bother to tell me until now."

"I figured the poor girl needed a bite to eat."

Tom's mentioning it seemed to make it so. My stomach growled. I *was* hungry.

"Poor girl!" hollered Lavern. "This *poor* girl's a stowaway. A common thief as far as I'm concerned."

"I am no thief," I argued. "I come equipped to pay my own way to California with cash money."

Lavern's voice softened. "How much cash money?"

I eyed him carefully. Tom, too. I remembered the gun. Would they take all my money and leave me stranded?

"Enough!" I told him.

Squinting through his ratty eyeglasses, Lavern stuck out his grimy paw. "Give it here. The money."

I took a step back. They were robbers!

Tom put his hand on my shoulder. "Keep your money, missy. Lavern here don't need it."

Lavern coughed. "Don't need it? This little bandit got herself a free ride."

"A ride in the back of this run-down pickup under a stinking sheet of canvas ain't worth no more than free."

Lavern just huffed and stomped off to the front of the truck. He lifted the hood and peered at the engine.

I sighed in relief, then told Tom, "Thank you, sir, for your kindness."

"Weren't none given," he answered. "I just don't like to see Lavern rule the roost. He's been sour since we left Kansas City."

I studied the landscape, trying to get an idea of where we might be. Nowhere would have been a good name for

it. Flat as an iron griddle. The ground and sky both dull
brown. Here and there a few gray, pokey-looking bushes
broke up the flatness. Off in the distance tumbleweeds
scooted across the dusty land till they snagged them-
selves against a barbed wire fence. I guessed this to be
the flatlands of Oklahoma or Texas.

The sun tried to burn a hole in the brown sky in the
west. Nearly dusk already? I had slept a long time.

Tom fetched a shovel from the back of the pickup. He
dug a shallow hole and dropped in some scraps of wood
he'd taken from a burlap bag. Then he started a fire.

He asked, "What's your name?"

"Jessica Whitney Land. My friends call me Jessie."

"I'm Tom McCauley. That miserable cuss up there's
Lavern Brewster. We're related somehow, I'm sorry to
say."

Lavern slammed the hood closed and tramped back to
the fire. With his lip stuck out like a pouting child, he
made me think of Walter Scott Tyler, my cousin.

"Lavern hails from Kansas City," Tom went on. "His
folks died last year. They left him this pickup and some
pots and dishes and such from a little café they owned
before the Depression."

"I don't see no need to tell this stowaway the story of
my life," Lavern complained.

Ignoring him, Tom added more wood to the fire. From
the heavy, cardboard box in the back of the pickup he
fished out a black cast-iron pot and some cans. Then he
quickly prepared a meal.

Before long the smell of beans spread around us at the fire. My head felt light from hunger so when Tom offered me a plate of hot beans, I nearly yanked it from his hands. Beans never much appealed to me before, but at that moment they tasted as good as anything Mama served at Sunday dinner.

After we finished, Tom showed me how to scrub the dishes shiny with water and sand. This was truly educational. I'd never heard of such a thing! The plates and pot gleamed when he finished.

"It's the way we used to wash up as cowboys," he explained, "even when water couldn't be found."

"You were a *cowboy?*" I asked, impressed.

"Yep. I worked some herds, drove a bunch of cows north, and spent time minding some line camps. But that was a long time ago. Before. . . ."

Abruptly, he glanced at me.

He turned away. Before what? I wanted to ask him, but I kept still.

After Tom packed the last plate away in the cardboard box, Lavern spoke up, "I say we keep driving. We can make Amarillo early tomorrow."

"There's no rush," Tom insisted. "That loot's not going anywhere."

"*Shhh!*" Lavern leaped up from his seat on a large rock. "Can't you keep your old man mouth shut for once?"

What a scoundrel this Lavern was! I declared, "Mr. Brewster, the Bible teaches us to *respect* our elders."

Lavern dropped back down to the rock, his mouth gaping. Some folks seem surprised to learn that I hold opinions.

Tom stroked his white mustache and cackled.

"Don't encourage her!" Lavern cried. "She's got enough salt in her as it is." He wagged a finger at me. "Girlie, you may've ridden this far. You may've eaten our beans and warmed yourself by our fire. You may even be sleeping here tonight. But come morning you'll be hitching your way back along the dusty road to Liberal. I *guarantee* you that."

I shivered at his words. All I could think about was how would I ever reach Mama and Daddy in time if I were put out here. He couldn't leave me here. He just couldn't.

With that warning, Lavern yanked out a blanket from the truck bed and climbed inside the cab.

Tom silently spread a couple blankets for me in the truck bed and laid another for himself on the ground.

I tugged the blanket up over my head and tried to forget Lavern's threat. When I finally fell asleep, I had strange and awful dreams about both Lavern and Aunt Edna.

*   *   *

I woke to morning smells — the smoky fire, strong coffee, and something cooking. The air seemed fresher, but when I looked south I knew it wouldn't last. A black blow headed our way.

Tom appeared from behind the pickup, tucking in his

purple shirttail. A bit of ragged towel hung draped over his shoulder. Flecks of shaving soap clung to his cheeks.

He smiled. "Mornin', Jessie."

I smiled right back. "Good morning, Mr. McCauley."

"Call me Tom." He worked at his pale face with the towel.

I climbed out of the truck bed and stretched. My back ached from sleeping on metal, and I was covered with dust.

"I saved you some beans and a bit of salt pork and a splash of coffee for breakfast," he informed me.

Beans and salt pork for breakfast? Well, it would be a first for me.

I warmed myself beside the campfire. Wisps of gray smoke curled into the brown sky. This place reminded me of Liberal. The same brown sky with a blow headed our way.

I took a swig of coffee. It tasted bitter. I swished it around in my mouth and spit it out to get rid of the sand and grit on my teeth. Then I went after the pork and beans, all jumbled together in a burned tin can. I ate it all. In fact, I ate it before I remembered to say grace. And this was Sunday, the Lord's day!

Shamed and with food still in my mouth, I bowed my head and started a silent prayer of late thanks.

Lavern interrupted before I got to "Amen."

"Well, girlie, now that you're finished eating our grub, I'll point you down the road. Liberal is a ways back."

The food I'd swallowed felt like a rock in my stomach. I

grew cold and started shivering.

Tom said, "Lavern, I told you last night she's goin' with us."

I dropped the empty can into the burning embers and stood up, wrapping my arms around me. I looked from Lavern to Tom and then back to Lavern. They gazed at each other, paying me no mind. Beyond them, the blow kept sweeping toward us.

"I know what you said," Lavern argued.

"We're not setting this child loose out here."

"And why not?"

"She's just a kid. I had a daughter once, you know."

"What's that gotta do with anything?" Lavern answered.

"If you don't take her along, *I* won't go along. And if I don't go, you don't get the loot."

Lavern shook his head and jammed his fists into his pockets. "That's extortion," he said through gritted teeth.

"Call it what you like."

The lump in my stomach began to disappear. This argument seemed to be about something beside me. What was this loot business?

"You're bluffing," Lavern sputtered.

Tom took three steps toward the other man. He said, "Just try me."

They stood face to face like old-time gunfighters. Then the big, black cloud of dust swept in. The grit pelted my face, stinging my eyes. I yanked my bandanna up to cover my mouth and nose. I could barely see. I heard Tom and Lavern coughing. For the second time I felt grateful for a dust storm. It put a quick end to their argument.

"Aw, get in the pickup," Lavern wheezed. "She can ride to the next stopping place. But that's it."

Tom took my hand and yanked me after him. I grabbed Marjorie and my bundle of possessions from the truck bed and started to climb into the cab.

I stopped short. Perched on the seat, sat a *skunk!*

I stepped back, but Tom nudged me on.

"Don't mind the critter, it's just Lavern's pet," he explained. "She's safe. Born without a stink sack."

I edged over on the seat, my eyes fixed on the skunk. How'd he know she didn't have a stink sack? Maybe she just hadn't used it yet. The skunk gave me a brief glance before climbing onto Lavern's lap.

Lavern rubbed the skunk's head and murmured, "That's my Juniper."

A skunk named Juniper. Imagine it! I suppose you could put a name to anything, but that didn't change the thing. Adam could've named skunks roses and roses skunks. It wouldn't have done a thing to the smell of either one, though I guess the skunks would've appreciated it.

Lavern grumbled as the engine shuddered and finally caught. He let it warm up a bit. Then he worked the clutch and the pickup jerked back onto the road.

My heart jumped. Here I went. Toward California and Mama and Daddy! I tried not to think about Lavern's threat to leave me at the next stopping place.

The rest of that morning faded into a blur. Every once

in a while we'd see another car stopped alongside the road or a tumbleweed whipping by or someone with his thumb out, hopeful for a ride. Always there was the dust, the reddish-brown sky, and the smell of sweat.

I jumped when Juniper crawled into my lap. She nuzzled my hand. The creature seemed to like me.

When I looked out the windshield, I saw nothing but barren land. It was no place to be without a ride.

"Used to do a lot of riding around here," Tom told me.

"Yeah, Tennessee Tom, wasn't this where Billy the Kid and your other pals rode the old outlaw trail?" Lavern asked. He snickered like some pesky schoolboy.

I didn't understand. What did Tom have to do with Billy the Kid? What did Lavern mean by "rode the outlaw trail"? And why'd he call Tom "Tennessee Tom"?

Tom just ignored him.

"Hey, girlie, speaking of trails, up ahead is the end of the trail for you," Lavern announced. "From now on, you can mooch off someone else."

The lump in my stomach returned as I stared out the windshield. Up ahead a large sagging sign read, LAWSON'S GAS AND CURIO. Beneath it I saw two faded red gas pumps and a small tin building. Not much of a place.

Would Lavern really put me out? Today was Sunday. I had only five more days to get to California. Please, God, don't let him put me out *here!*

Chapter 4

Tom ignored Lavern's threat. "I'm ready to stop a spell myself," he admitted. "I need to stretch my legs."

I looked hard at him, trying to figure out if he was for me or against me. But he turned away and gazed at the gas station.

I stuck my hand into my pocket and clutched Mama's letter. She had prayed for a guardian angel for me. It didn't look like I could count on either of these men as an answer to that prayer.

As the pickup slowed, Lavern sassed me. "If your luck holds out, you little scalawag, there oughta be another California-bound sucker along in a week or so."

A wave of fear shook me, but I swallowed hard, trying to be brave. "I don't believe in luck, Mr. Brewster. And I don't appreciate you calling me a 'scalawag.'"

Lavern just grunted as the pickup skidded to a stop beside the gas pumps.

The two men got out of the cab. I eased the sleeping skunk off my lap.

Tom and Lavern went inside the tin building. Glancing around, I felt a rush of panic. What could I do? Five days to get to California. I needed a ride—*now*.

A tall, red-headed woman in khaki coveralls stooped beside the only other car around. A parked car facing west!

Clutching my bundle of possessions, I walked over. The woman was digging through a large metal box.

"Could you use some help?" I offered.

She was very pretty. Nearly as pretty as Mama, but her hair looked like mine. Or the way my hair used to look. Instead of down, though, she wore her long red hair swept up on top of her head. Her green eyes sparkled. When she smiled at me, I saw a row of perfect white teeth. Lovely white.

"Hi there," she said. "Did you say something?"

She talked crisply, not like the country people I knew.

"Could you use some help?" I repeated, pointing at the metal box.

"Oh, no, that's all right. I've got it. Just my camera equipment."

She held up a small, black contraption that I took to be a camera.

"You take pictures?" I asked her.

She nodded and stood up. I'd never met a picture-taker before, much less a lady picture-taker. I'd also never met anyone who looked so attractive in coveralls. She had a wide, friendly smile, and her eyes remained on me. Like she was interested in me.

She stretched out her hand and said, "I'm Alice Townes. From Los Angeles."

Los Angeles! Could this be my guardian angel at last?

Seeing her small, clean hand, I felt ashamed at how dirty I was. My neck was grimy, and my butchered hair smelled like a campfire. After sleeping in my clothes, they looked dirty and wrinkled. I wished I had at least changed my shirt. All the same, I wiped my hand on my overalls and took hers. You didn't turn down a handshake with an angel, even a possible angel.

"Jessie Land. From Liber—Bound for California."

Alice Townes' smile faded a little. "I've met quite a few families going to California."

"Mama and Daddy are already there," I explained. "I'm on my way to join them. I've been traveling with those men." I pointed out Tom and Lavern standing beside the tin building. "They're headed for Harvest-of-Gold, California."

"Harvest-of-Gold?"

"It's not far from San Bernardino, I gather," I explained to her.

"What an unusual name," she said. "I've never heard of it."

She had a kind face, so I told her about our sharecropper's farm in southeastern Oklahoma. About the drought. About the cotton crop failing and then the farm getting sold. About staying with the Tylers. I left out the part about running away.

She frowned. "Why didn't your parents just take you with them?"

I couldn't tell her the real reason. I hadn't even told

Tom that. I felt too ashamed.

"They figured it'd be easier until they got settled."

It wasn't a lie. It just wasn't the whole truth.

"What do you think California's like?" she asked.

I knew right away how to describe it. "The sky's bright blue. And fruits and vegetables grow everywhere. Imagine a place called Harvest-of-Gold! The houses are all so white they sparkle under the sun." And, I thought to myself, Mama and Daddy are there. That was the most important part.

"Is it like that?" I asked Alice Townes.

"I live in the city. But, yes, it's . . . it's, well, a lot like you dreamed it to be."

Her eyes slid away from me. I could tell she wasn't telling the whole truth herself.

"You don't need to say that because I'm young," I said. "I'm not a child. You can speak your mind."

She looked at me in surprise. When she answered, she kept her eyes on mine.

"People are out of work and hungry there too, Jessie. And now people are streaming in from all over the country. For some reason people seem to think of California as the promised land. California may not have dust storms, but it has its own share of troubles."

"The Lord said if you live in the world you'll face trouble," I told Alice Townes. "Trouble doesn't bother me. Dust storms don't even bother me any more. I just want to be with Mama and Daddy."

"Then I hope you find them soon."

I looked back. Tom was checking the green canvas covering the truck bed. Lavern cursed as he tried to straighten a twisted water hose. An old car loaded high with furniture and other stuff rocked in off the road and skidded to a stop behind the pickup.

I turned back to Alice Townes, closed my eyes for a second, and said a silent prayer. *Please, God, let her really be the guardian angel Mama asked you for.*

When I opened my eyes, I asked, hopeful, "Are you headed back home?"

She brushed back a strand of loose red hair from in front of her eyes. "To L.A.? Yes, I am."

"Would you be willing to take me as far as San Bernardino? I can pay you three dollars."

I watched her eyes, hopeful she wouldn't turn me down. She seemed to be sizing me up. Maybe even asking herself, what if this dirty child is a thief?

"I thought you were riding with those men," she said.

"Not any more."

"Oh." She smiled slightly. "Well, you're welcome to come as far as Amarillo. I'm flying from there to Los Angeles."

I felt suddenly empty. Amarillo. That was just Texas. I needed to get a lot farther than Texas. Still, though, Amarillo was down the road a ways, and I'd gone as far as I could with Tom and Lavern.

"I'd be happy to go to Amarillo with you," I told her.

Alice Townes started to load the metal box into her car. She turned and said, "Do you mind if I take your picture before we leave?"

My heart fluttered. I'd never had my picture taken before. "No, ma'am, I don't mind at all."

The fact was I thought pretty highly of the idea.

She had me stand beside the highway next to a sign in the shape of a pointing hand that read *This way to Route 66.*

After she'd taken a few pictures, I climbed beside her in the front seat, my bundle on my lap. She wrote my name in a little notebook she kept on the seat. I didn't know whether to feel happy or upset. I was on my way, but it would be a short trip with Alice Townes. Then I thought about Tom. I sort of missed him already. Glancing back, I spied him beside the pickup. He was calling my name, looking for me.

I turned to Alice Townes. She started the car. Tom's voice crackled in the dry air. *"Jessie!"*

He must have convinced Lavern to take me with them. I didn't care much for Lavern's company, but something inside told me to stick with the ride I started with.

"I'm sorry, ma'am," I told Alice Townes. "It looks like I have a ride already." I climbed out of her car.

"You sure?" she asked.

Nodding, I said, "Thanks for your kindness."

Sadness seemed to glow in those green eyes. She smiled. "Good luck, Jessie Land."

"I don't believe in luck," I answered for the second time that day. "But thanks all the same."

I took off for Tom.

"God bless you then," she called out after me.

I joined Tom beside the pickup. He held out an old, cracked cup.

"I was looking for you," he said. "Care for some water?"

"Thanks." I took a sip. It tasted warm and I noticed sand at the bottom of the cup. I drank it down anyway.

"Can't seem to get enough to drink," Tom said. "Bein' out in this dust and wind is just like when I rode drag on a big cattle drive. All the herd in front of me stirrin' up the earth. I'd come in covered with a half inch of dust. And I could never get enough water to drink then."

Much as I wanted to hear about his cowboy past, my mind was set on other things.

I asked, "How'd you talk Lavern into letting me ride with you?"

Tom patted my back. "I'm sorry, Jessie. I didn't. He's mule-stubborn. Said he won't take you one more mile."

"*What?*" I cried. I spun around.

Alice Townes' car pulled onto the highway and drove off. I started to run after her, but it was no use.

Oh, dear Lord.

Chapter 5

"I tried, Jessie, to change his mind," Tom said. "I did get him to agree we'd find you another ride. We won't just leave you stranded."

He didn't understand that I had had a ride. I could have been on my way! Alice Townes might've even offered me a ride on that airplane to California!

I shook my head, furious at myself for getting out of Alice Townes' car. *You brainless little fool,* I told myself. Hot tears burned in my eyes. I rubbed them away. It was a bigger fool who thought she could solve anything by crying. But the idea of being handed off to other strangers made me feel helpless. So far, at least, I'd picked my own rides.

I watched Lavern finish adding water to the radiator. Then he turned off the spigot and went over to a man beside the loaded-down car. The two of them squatted in the dust, their backs to me. Their voices buzzed low in the dry air. I didn't trust Lavern. He'd dump me on anyone. I edged closer so I could hear their words.

The other man was talking.

". . . and then after that the bank in Coldwater fore-closed on us."

I knew Coldwater to be a small town in Kansas. Uncle Rudy's brother lived there.

"The car's not been very reliable," he continued. "Broke down three or four times already. I'm not sure we'll make it all the way to California. Likely we'll end up in New Mexico or Arizona somewheres."

"That's too bad," Lavern told him. He sounded genuine enough. "There's a lot of people on the road these days. Just yesterday we picked up this little orphan girl. She told us she was an orphan anyway. Imagine that. A child out hitching a ride. She really needs to be with a family and not with a couple of old coots like us."

Orphan! And he had called me a scalawag! I saw through his words at once. He was trying to dump me on this poor family who didn't even have enough money to be on the road in the first place.

"How old is she?" the man asked.

"Nine or ten I guess," Lavern replied. "Name's Jenny."

Jenny! Nine or ten! He lacked character, suffered from a terrible memory, and was a poor judge of children's ages!

"My wife always wanted a girl," the other man confessed. "We got us four boys."

I could almost hear wheels spinning in Lavern's head.

"Listen, Mac, maybe I could help you out some," he began. "If you'd be willing to take this poor little orphan girl, I might be able to give you a little something for your trouble."

"Give me what?"

"I got me a bit of corn meal and some salt pork I could spare. That'd help you out some. And girls don't eat much. This one hardly eats nothin'."

Especially if you don't feed her anything except beans and salty meat! I fumed.

Then I realized I needed a plan quick or I'd be traded off to this family and wind up in Arizona. I don't know why but the first thing that came to mind involved a bare-faced lie.

I stalked in front of them and looked straight at Lavern. His face turned blood red.

"Daddy, when're we gonna go?" I pleaded.

The other man turned his craggy face on Lavern.

"Daddy? Is this the girl? You said 'orphan.' What are you up to, mister? You tryin' to get rid of your own child?"

I giggled.

"Did Daddy try that again?" I asked the man. "He's always trying to pawn me off on someone. Ever since I got that sickness."

"Sickness!" cried the man, his eyes wide. He jumped up and away from both of us. "What in tarnation's going on here?" His eyes blazed at Lavern. "You oughta be turned in to the po-lice, mister."

The man scurried toward his car.

From behind his bent spectacles Lavern's black eyes glared at me. "You think you're real funny, don't you?"

I shook my head. "No. I'm just looking out for myself since I can't trust you to."

"Why should I look out after you?" he asked. "Am I your father? Do I owe you anything? *You're* the one that snuck on board my pickup."

"And for that you're gonna trade me off to that poor family?"

"I shouldn't even stop to talk to you, girlie," he said with a sneer. "I oughta just leave you stranded out here."

The thought of that made me feel cold and empty. I swallowed hard and said, "I'll give you a dollar to take me a bit farther on."

Lavern rubbed his dirty cheek and licked his lips. He squeezed his two hands together. I never saw a man get so worked up over gaining a dollar.

"How much farther?"

"To the next stopping place."

He stuck out his grimy hand. I went over to my bundle and fetched a dollar from my Bible, making sure neither Lavern nor Tom could see. Tom just gazed at me, puzzled.

When I laid the dollar in Lavern's hand, he didn't say thanks. His fingers curled tightly over the bill and he growled, "Let's go."

We traveled a while in silence. Juniper contented herself lying on the floor under Lavern's feet. When I got tired watching the flat land and the acres of dust, I asked Tom, "How old is your daughter?"

He was a pale man by anyone's standards, but he became paler still.

He shook his head. "It was a long time ago, Jessie. She'd be about forty-four if she's still livin'."

Still living! "You don't even know if she's alive?"

"Nope, her mother neither," he admitted.

"Well, when did you last see them?"

" 'Bout forty-three years ago."

"How could that be?"

Lavern snickered and Tom said, "Hush up, Lavern."

"Just tell her what a great family man you once were, Tennessee Tom," Lavern said with a sneer.

Tom ignored his kin and told me, "Jessie, people have their disagreements and their troubles. It's just history. Old unhappy history. That's all."

I wanted to know more, but he didn't want to talk about it. So I said, "Are you from Tennessee?"

That stirred up Lavern. With a mighty guffaw, he nearly threw us into a ditch.

"Keep the vehicle on the road," complained Tom.

"I don't see what's so funny," I said.

"That's because you don't know everything like you think you do," Lavern sassed. "Go ahead, Tom. Tell her about your Tennessee roots."

He laughed again, but this time he seemed to have a little more control over himself and the pickup.

"I was born in Tennessee, Jessie," Tom explained. "It's just a nickname, that's all."

"*All?*" Lavern cackled.

I paid no mind to Lavern's obnoxious behavior and asked Tom, "What did you mean this morning—that talk about loot?"

All at once Lavern hammered his fists against the

steering wheel. He exploded, *"See there!* Your casual remarks are remembered by this so-called mere child." He shook his finger at me and threatened, "You just forget anyone ever used the word *loot.* Understand? This don't concern you at all."

Tom cleared his throat and said quietly, "The loot I mentioned—"

"Tom!" shrieked Lavern.

"Hush, Lavern. The loot is—ah—well, it's really gold. It's in a lost mine in California. I know this old bird there who says he has a map. We're gonna help him find it. That's all."

I thought about what he said. It didn't make a whole lot of sense. "If this other man's got the map, why does he need you? Why doesn't he just dig up the gold himself?"

This idea never seemed to have occurred to Tom. After a moment he answered, "It takes money to mine for gold. Equipment, supplies, and such. This man needs us because we've got the supplies and the money to help grubstake him."

Somehow this didn't sound quite right to me either. Why would someone with a real gold mine map need to get help from halfway across the country?

I remembered the handgun in the truck bed. And the talk about "the outlaw trail," Billy the Kid, and a lost wife and daughter. *What were these men really up to?*

* * *

At Amarillo we turned west onto Route 66. Driving
through the rest of Texas was like cruising along the top
of a table.

New Mexico seemed strange with its flat-topped hills.
It was even drier and dustier than the place I'd left. Every
so often a dust blow would sweep past, rocking the pickup, the sand and dirt scratching against metal and glass.
The sky became bluer, with thin, brown clouds drifting
across it.

Hazy, gray shapes flecked with white appeared in the
distance. I started to ask Tom about them, but he
slumped next to me, asleep. His head rested against the
window. He blew a foggy breath on the glass.

The shapes grew larger. They looked like herd of pur-
ply-gray elephants. The white flecks became their tusks,
jutting out from their huge heads.

Then, at some point, they changed. I saw them for
what they truly were. Mountains. Mountains with snow
on top! I'd only seen such things in picture books and I
couldn't take my eyes off them. My heart raced. I wanted
to shake Tom awake so he could see them too.

I turned to Lavern. *"Look at those mountains!"*

His head jolted and he let loose a wild cry. *"Mmmr-
whaaa!"* He jerked the wheel and the pickup veered
across the road in a sudden swerve.

We headed straight for a gulch!

"Look out!" I shrieked.

Chapter 6

Lavern stomped on the brake. We started spinning, as if the pickup had turned itself into a dust devil.

When we finally rocked to a stop, we faced the way we had just come. The mountains loomed behind us. We were both breathing hard.

A groggy Tom muttered, "What—? What's happening?"

"You little nincompoop!" exploded Lavern. "You nearly got us killed!"

"Me?" I shot back. "You were asleep at the wheel. If I hadn't spoken, we would've gone off the road and been crushed like peas in a tin can."

"I was not sleeping," Lavern protested. "Just resting. Until you screamed in my ear."

"That's nonsense and you know it."

"Now, now, no harm done," Tom said to quiet both of us. "Let's just keep going."

Grumbling, Lavern turned the pickup around and headed us in the right direction.

I took a deep breath, closed my eyes, and said a silent prayer of thanks for God's protection.

It grew dark before we reached a small town. My stom-

ach growled, but what I really longed for was a place to lie
down.

We found a nice little park in the center of town. All
three of us collapsed on a bench.

Guitar music drifted in the dark, cold air. "Where can
we sleep?" I asked Tom.

"We don't have money for a hotel—if there is one in
this place," he confessed. "I say let's find us an out-of-
the-way place to get some sleep."

"I'd give a lot for a good meal and a bath," I admitted.

"When you joined this party, you gave up luxuries like
baths and regular meals," Lavern mumbled. "Of course,
now that we've reached civilization, you're on your own
as far as I'm concerned. Mooch off someone else for a
change."

I shivered at his words, but looked at a certain way I
was a moocher. I had stowed away on the pickup. Maybe
it was time to leave these men.

I stood up and started to walk toward . . . toward what?
I didn't know. But I hadn't taken ten steps when Tom
pulled alongside me. I felt relieved at the sight of him.

"Where're you going, missy?" he asked, grabbing my
arm.

"I don't know. Find some place to lie down I guess."

"Well, we'd better stick together," he remarked. "I
don't much like the idea of your wandering around alone."

"What about Lavern?"

"He's asleep on the bench," Tom said. "No one'll bother a man keeping company with a skunk."

We came to a small stream and decided to camp there. I lay on a thin, rough blanket near the water. Tom draped his coat over me. I wondered how I would ever get to California now. I saw Mama's face in my mind. Her smile. My heart ached. I missed her and Daddy so bad. Mama, why did you and Daddy have to leave me behind? *Why?*

Tom took up a position beside a scrawny bush a little ways off and went right to sleep. I listened to his heavy snoring and to night birds chittering in the sky. I pulled Tom's coat tight around me against the cold night air.

Then I prayed, *Dear Lord, I'm stuck here in New Mexico. Please send that guardian angel to help me get to California. Please, Lord, get me to Mama and Daddy in time!*

* * *

I woke as the sun burst up all red and fierce, chasing off the sparkling stars and the half moon. The stream bubbled and the crisp, cool air made me shiver beneath Tom's coat.

Remembering my prayer from the night before, I glanced around, hoping to spy my guardian angel coming to rescue me and whisk me off to California. But all I saw was a dusty street and pinkish, flat-topped buildings.

I got up and went over to Tom. His black hat covered his face. His breathing came in deep, heavy sighs. His pale, wrinkled hands jerked at his sides. Glancing down at his polished green boots, I noticed something white poking out of his boot heel. I stooped to examine it, but the sound of a car made me turn around.

A black pickup clattered up the street.

Lavern.

When the pickup squealed to a stop, Lavern scrunched up his face at me and said, "You found anybody else you can steal a ride with, girlie?"

The man was so offensive! His words struck at me. I had to do something. I couldn't be left behind here.

I got up and went over to him.

"What if I were to pay you another dollar," I offered.

"Two dollars to the next stop," he replied, his dirty palm out.

"One dollar, Mr. Brewster, when we stop."

He gave it some thought, looking all the more unpleasant for it. Finally, he said, "Well, wake up that old coot, so we can get going."

I didn't need to wake Tom. He was up. He joined me beside the car.

Lavern took off his spectacles and tried wiping them on his shirt. They came apart in his hands. *"Drat!"* He worked at putting them back together, then shoved them up on his dirty face.

We climbed in the pickup. Already Lavern had burdened the cab with the smell of sweat.

As we headed out of the little town, I noticed a beautiful old church. Tom said it was made of adobe which wasn't anything more than mud. I'd seen a sod house before, back in Kansas. I couldn't quite imagine folks worshiping in a mud church, even a pink mud church.

The pickup rattled down the quiet Monday morning street. It made me think. Today was Monday. Four days left to reach Mama and Daddy.

We reached Albuquerque before noon and continued west on Route 66. Knowing California lay straight ahead, though many miles, cheered me.

After a while, Tom passed around a jar of water and some thick slices of bread from a large, round loaf, the same thing we'd eaten for breakfast. When he handed me a slice, Lavern grumbled.

"What's eatin' you?" Tom asked him.

Lavern cleared his throat and said, "How much free food are you gonna let her stuff into her belly?"

"Oh, yeah, Lavern," replied Tom. "Lessee. We paid, what, a nickel for this two-day-old loaf? A slice of that oughta run Jessie, oh, about a half cent."

I laughed.

Nudging me with his elbow, Lavern spat, "What're you laughing at, you scamp?"

"I'll laugh when something strikes me funny," I told him.

His knuckles whitened on the steering wheel, but he didn't speak.

After that unpleasant conversation, the trip got better, mainly because Lavern stayed angry and pouted, refusing to talk.

I held my bundle in my lap, and after a while I reached in and took out Marjorie and my magazine pictures. I tucked my doll under my arm and spread the pictures across my lap, studying each one. Soon I felt Tom's eyes.

I gazed up at him. He wore a broad smile that forced a ripple of wrinkles on each side of his mouth.

"That's quite a collection."

I nodded in agreement. They'd been clipped from magazines given to me by Mr. Stevenson, Liberal's barber. Most Fridays, after school, I'd stop at the barber shop. Mr. Stevenson would have a stack of magazines ready for me along with a pair of scissors. I'd go through each one, sometimes cutting out a dozen pictures, sometimes not cutting a one. All of them ended up in a shoebox under my bed at the Tylers. In that crazy, last-minute decision to leave, I'd only brought the special pictures. The ones I kept separate in my corner of a drawer.

"That one looks like Wyoming or Montana," Tom remarked, pointing.

I nodded, touching the corners of one picture lightly so I wouldn't get fingerprints on it. "Right! It's a sky in Montana. See, just a few clouds, and all of them white. I'll bet that blue sky is something to look at, don't you?"

I had to imagine. All the pictures were black and white.

"Uh-huh. What about this one here?" he asked.

"That's a picture from somebody's trip to the North Pole. I cut it out because it seems so strange. Imagine seeing nothing but white everywhere you look."

As much as I liked the North Pole picture, it wasn't my favorite.

"Here's the one I like best," I told him. I felt Lavern's eyes too.

"That house is a beauty," Tom admitted. "And big."

"Yes." I sighed as I looked at the picture.

The house stood big and white and pretty in the middle of a field of mowed grass. No dust or threatening clouds. Like always, tears came to my eyes when I saw the family sitting together on the wide porch swing. My heart ached because it could've been Mama and Daddy and me.

"Lemme see that picture," came Lavern's sudden voice, and just as sudden his grimy fingertips. He plucked the picture from my grasp.

"Give it back!" I shrieked at him.

The scoundrel jerked his hand away from my reaching arms and steered the pickup with his right hand alone. With his left hand he held the picture close to the window and looked it over.

"Give that picture back!" I screamed again.

"Calm yourself, girlie," he told me.

I couldn't help myself. I grabbed hold of his sleeve and yanked hard. The pickup veered right, nearly plunging us down a gully.

"Hey!" Lavern cried.

"Give it back! *Give it back!*" I shouted at him.

"You're gonna throw us in that ditch, you little fool," he growled.

"Give her back the picture," Tom said quietly.

"Why should I?"

Tom reached over me and snapped the picture out of Lavern's fingers. He smiled and dropped it in my lap.

Where the nasty Lavern had clutched it a large wrinkle

and a dark smudge ruined the picture. Now there appeared to be a heavy, gray cloud hovering over the house.

Anger rose up inside me. I knew I should keep quiet but I blurted out, "You are spiteful, Lavern Brewster. You've got a root of bitterness in you. Stop this truck!"

Lavern looked dumbfounded.

"Stop this truck now!" I cried out.

Then, scowling at Tom and me, he slammed on the brakes and skidded the pickup over to the side of the road.

I held the picture up to his face. "Look what you did. A huge smudge. You *ruined* it. I want out. Right now."

Tom didn't budge. Lavern just stared at me.

"Get out and let me out!" I insisted. "I want out."

Lavern opened the door and crawled out.

"Jessie . . ." Tom began.

"I've had enough of—of *him,*" I fumed at Tom. "He's the most vile person I ever met. I can't take him anymore."

I tore out, clutching my bundle in my arms. My heart thundered in my chest. I wondered if I knew what I was doing. No, probably not. But I was too angry.

Lavern just stood beside the pickup, gaping at me then bending down and gaping at Tom, inside the cab.

I gave Lavern a final glance and said, "As you said to me once, 'good riddance!' " Then I set out on the road. *What are you doing? So proud you're willing to give up your ride?*

Behind me I heard Tom say, "Well, I reckon I'll get out

too. She's right, Lavern, you are vile."

"Wait, Tom, don't go," Lavern said. "It's her. It's that little troublemaker who's to blame."

I turned and saw Tom grab at some bundles in the truck bed.

"Tom, get back in," Lavern demanded. "Don't you see? We were doing fine till this little stowaway snuck on."

"She's never been no trouble," Tom announced. "You're the only trouble. Maybe driving to California all by yourself will teach you to appreciate folks."

With that, Tom joined me and we trudged off down the road, leaving Lavern beside the truck.

My anger finally died. I glanced up at Tom. He stared straight ahead. I wondered if he was thinking the same thing as me. How were we going to get to California now?

Chapter 7

All I could think about as Tom and I began our trek toward California on foot was: *You little fool! You had a ride and you gave it up. What were you thinking? Maybe Aunt Edna was right—all you ever seemed to do was cause trouble.*

Just then, I heard the pickup start up. We were off to the side of the road a bit, our shoes stirring up the dust. The sun burned the top of my head and I wished I had a hat. The sound of the pickup's engine grew louder and louder. Soon it sounded like some kind of roaring monster coming up behind us. Tom just seemed to ignore the noise, but it gave me a creepy feeling. I turned around to look.

The pickup was headed straight for us!

I saw Lavern hunched over the wheel, jerking it from side to side. Enormous clouds of dust rose on both sides of the truck, just like some horrible blow. A blow that could knock you down and crush you!

"Look out!" I cried. *"The truck!"*

Tom jerked around. The truck came at us fast.

Tom swooped me up in his strong arms. I seemed to be

flying, but slow-like. Then he threw me out of the path of the pickup, sending me sprawling in the dust and weeds at the side of the road.

The pickup whizzed past, raising another huge cloud of sand and dirt. After the dust cleared, I looked up to see the truck spinning around like a crazy compass needle. It skidded sideways and rocked to a stop, its nose aimed at us.

My heart pounded. I felt like I couldn't breathe. I jumped up, my fear turning to fire inside me.

"That scoundrel tried to run us over!" I cried.

"That seemed to be his intent," Tom remarked, dusting himself off.

Tom stalked off toward the pickup. But before he got too close Lavern turned the vehicle around and tore out, the tires spewing more dirt and sand.

"Lavern!" Tom cried. "Come back here!"

Lavern ripped down the road at a furious speed.

"That man is *crazy,*" I said, catching up to Tom.

"He's one nasty cuss all right," Tom replied.

Watching the dusty cloud, I thought, *I'll never forgive him for treating me so mean. And for nearly killing us!*

But much as I might've wanted to consider his weaknesses, I had a more important subject on my mind. California. I had four days to get there and no ride.

The late afternoon sun hammered down on us. I don't know how many miles we walked, but the road stretched out in both directions for what seemed like forever. Here and there a clump of cactus or sagebrush poked up out of

the dry, dusty ground. We had no water and the prospects
of coming across some didn't look good. Sweat streamed
off my face and dripped on my shirt and overalls. I wiped
my face with my arm, leaving a wet, dirty mark on my
sleeve. I thought about the water jug in the car.

"You know, on a hot day like this, a swig of cactus milk
would taste mighty good," Tom suggested, as if he could
read my mind.

He tramped over to a fat cactus that stood taller than
him. With a pocket knife he hacked at the middle of it.

He brought me a sizeable chunk of cactus. He mashed
the pulp inside with his knife. When he held the cactus
out, I noticed red splotches in his palms where the needles had pricked him.

"Chew up that mess of pulp there, Jessie," he said.
"It's just chock full of milk."

"Milk?"

"Well, it's really water. The main thing's it's wet."

I had a terrible thirst, but the cactus pulp didn't look
like anything I wanted to stick in my mouth. It resembled
a clump of spinach and I hated spinach. Tom nudged the
cactus at me.

"Go on, try it," he said. "It won't hurt you none. 'Cept
be sure you spit out the pulp after you're finished getting
all the juice out. Otherwise you might get a whale of a
bellyache."

I took a big bite and chewed. It tasted vile, but the
milk's wetness refreshed me. When I finished chewing, I
spit out a big wad of dark-green stuff.

I wiped the dripping milk from my chin and watched as Tom went back to the cactus to cut some for himself. It hit me then. Could *Tom* be my guardian angel? The answer to Mama's prayer? Somehow he wasn't what I expected, but he'd certainly looked after me. From the very first.

We set out again. Up the road a piece we came upon the smashed body of an armadillo, a big one. The tire marks looked like someone had pretty much swerved over to the side of the road just to hit it.

Lavern! He'd driven off like such a wild man.

Just past the smashed body, I saw something wandering in circles beside the road. Rushing over, I got a better view. Tom came up behind me.

"Baby armadillo. Probably belonged to that squashed one back there. They're both nine-banded 'dillos."

"Do you think . . . Lavern ran over the mama?"

He shrugged. "Could have. Wouldn't be unlike him. He's never taken to critters, 'cept for that blasted skunk."

I bent to touch the baby and it curled up into a little ball. I picked it up and held it in my arms. Its outside felt leathery. As I stroked the creature, tears swam into my eyes. The poor thing was all alone. I knew what I needed to do.

"I'm going to adopt it," I announced.

"What?" Tom said, frowning.

"Lavern might've killed the mama." I thought, a little guiltily, that it was because of me that Lavern had driven off in a rage.

Tom squinted at me. "I'll warn you, missy, that little critter probably ain't been properly weaned. She might not make it herself. Besides, there's something funny about them being out here."

"What do you mean?"

"I never knew of any 'dillos this far west. It's almost like they've migrated for some reason."

"Well, then, I have to adopt it," I said. "It's headed west just like me."

"Suit yourself. So what're you gonna name it?"

I thought a moment. Then I said, "Victoria."

"Good name. It was my mother's."

I smiled at him and at my hard-plated charge resting on top of the bundle I held in my arms. The animal was cute in a funny kind of way.

"So what do armadillos eat?" I asked.

"Bugs and such," he replied, and we kept going.

A few cars passed us. Tom got it into his head to use his thumb to get us a ride. Several cars passed without even slowing. Of course, every one of them looked loaded down. Likely they couldn't handle any more passengers.

Still I worried. I had four days. I began to fear that I'd reach California too late to catch Mama and Daddy. Just then I looked up to see Tom hold out his thumb as a dark green pickup came up from behind us. Then I saw for myself that very vehicle slow to a stop. Praise God!

We hustled over to the pickup. The old man behind the wheel and the young girl beside him peered at us and didn't say a word.

Tom broke the silence. "Can you folks give us a ride?"

Squirming in his dark suit, the man nodded and pointed in back.

Relieved, we climbed into the truck bed and settled among a load of potatoes. For the next several miles we bounced around something awful. My jaws crashed together as the pickup took every bump. I held tight to Victoria for fear she'd fly out of my arms and get smashed in the road.

The little girl in the cab kept staring out the back window at us. She seemed especially interested in my new-found pet. I couldn't help but stare at her too. She wore a pretty pink dress and had a long ponytail. Her face had a clean, scrubbed look to it. It seemed like forever since I'd been clean and all dressed up.

We went on like that for some time. The sun eased down in the western sky. I glanced through the window of the cab. Over the head of the staring girl and through the windshield something caught my eye.

What was that? Something black. I looked again.

Lavern's pickup truck!

I shook Tom who napped beside me. *"Look!"* I cried.

Sleepy-eyed, he squinted at the road ahead. His jaw tightened. He stood up and hammered on the roof of the cab.

"Stop!" he shouted at the driver. *"Stop right here!"*

It took a few seconds before the old man seemed to understand. Then as the pickup slowed to a stop, we passed Lavern's vehicle.

Tom climbed out. I grabbed my bundle and jumped down after him. Victoria peeked her head out a bit, then curled back into a ball. I breathed hard like I'd just run a race. My anger flared up again. I wanted to go over to that truck and slap the man who'd just about run us down.

The pickup sat crossways in a heap of sagebrush, like it had skidded off the road. Other than the half-buried rear tires, it didn't look any worse than the last time we'd seen it. Something was strange though. I didn't see Lavern.

"Lavern!" Tom yelled. "Where in blazes are you?"

I ran over to the pickup. Tom stalked up to the driver's door and yanked the handle. When the door flew open, I saw Lavern sprawled across the front seat. He didn't move.

"Come outta there, you scoundrel," ordered Tom.

Tom stood with his hands on his hips. I could almost picture him in cowboy attire squaring off against some bad guy. I'd seen such things in Saturday serials in the moving picture house in Liberal.

Lavern didn't accept the challenge. He didn't move. He was covered from head to foot with dirt and sand.

My anger at the man eased. Was he hurt? Or dead?

"Tom, what's wrong with him?"

Lavern stirred. Then he sat up and crawled out of the truck, looking confused. His glasses hung from one ear and his face was caked with grime. What on earth had happened?

Behind us I heard screeching automobile tires. I looked

back. The old man in the green pickup tore away, probably deciding he wanted no part of this scene. The little girl with the curious eyes still stared out the back window.

Lavern slumped as he stood before us. Finally, he gazed up at Tom, and I noticed something glistening on his face. Could those be actual tears in his eyes?

"I should strike you down," Tom told his relative. "The nerve of you trying to run us down like that!"

Right away the old meanness came back into Lavern's face. Bitterness burned in those coal black eyes. His voice, although a little hoarse, still cracked like a whip.

"What did you expect? You ran out on *me!* You left me, your own blood kin, for the likes of *her!*" He waved his arm at me. "She's responsible for the ruination of this trip."

"Take a look at yourself, Lavern," Tom said. "Did she do *this* to you? Did she throw you off the road and cover you with filth? This's your doing."

Wide-eyed, Lavern stared back at Tom.

Shaking his head, Lavern said, " 'Twasn't me. I—I was driving and this—this blasted tumbleweed flew up and caught me unawares. I guess I—I don't know—I guess I jerked the wheel. Next thing I knew the pickup spun off the road."

"So how'd you get so covered with dirt?" Tom asked.

Lavern pointed at a shovel lying on the ground. "I tried to dig the pickup out."

"I wish we'd passed you by," Tom told him.

Lavern lashed out, "Well, why didn't you?"

"I'm a bigger fool than you, that's why. Now I guess we might as well get this truck dug out and keep goin'."

Lavern's mouth quivered. Maybe it wanted to smile, but he kept it in check.

From the truck bed Tom drew out a couple of canvas bags. He dumped the contents, mainly tools, onto the dusty ground. Then he told Lavern to dig out the dirt around the wheels. Lavern grumbled the whole time. The man never missed an opportunity to complain.

Once the dirt was cleared out, Tom called me over. I set down Victoria and my bundled possessions. Tom and I spread the canvas bags behind the wheels.

Tom ordered, "All right, Lavern, you get in front and push. Jessie, you can push from over here by me. I'll start her up and give her some gas."

Tom climbed behind the wheel and started the engine.

Lavern wiped his grimy hands on his grimy clothes and planted them on the front bumper. I grabbed hold of the door beside Tom.

"Here we go!" Tom shouted.

He revved up the engine and then put it in reverse. The pickup bolted backward, then rocked forward. I heard the rear wheels spinning in the dirt.

Tom stopped. "Again," he called out.

Once more the wheels spun. The pickup rocked back and forth, but it didn't go anywhere.

Lavern muttered and slammed his fists on the hood. Tom looked more determined than ever. I smiled at him. The glint in his eyes reminded me of Daddy.

"This dirt is *not* stoppin' me," he declared not so much to me but to the truck. He gave the pickup a shot of gas.

This time it rocked free from the little ditch the tires had dug. The truck sprang backward, bouncing into the air. Tom backed it onto the highway.

Turning, I spied Lavern, all stretched out facedown in the dirt. I guessed the vehicle had bolted out so fast and unexpected that he'd pitched forward. He squirmed like a swimmer on the surface of a mud lake. Unkind as it was to laugh at someone's misfortune, I couldn't help giggling.

Tom left the running pickup on the highway and joined me.

"Lavern," he sang out, "this's no time for a mud bath."

The other man just sat up with a scowl on his face as ornery as any I'd ever seen.

He spat out a mouthful of grit and choked, "You drive, Tom. I'm tired and fed up."

* * *

At dusk, we drove into Gallup, a good-sized town in western New Mexico. I watched folks standing on the sidewalks, some sitting down and leaning against the buildings. None of them looked too prosperous. On many of the buildings someone had painted unusual signs with Indian figures. One of the largest signs read: *Soup Kitchen—food for the unemployed available today.* I spotted a bank, its lights still on. I'd seen so many banks with *Foreclosed* painted across them that it seemed odd to see one still in business.

Tom suggested stopping a bit to check the water and oil. We were all plenty hungry too. I knew Lavern wouldn't offer to feed me, so I got my bundle and prepared to buy a sandwich or two.

When we stepped out of the truck to stretch our legs, we heard shouting. Something was up.

"Come on, missy," Tom said to me. "Let's see what's going on."

I grabbed Victoria and my bundle. Curious, I followed Tom. As we set out, the smell of fresh bread drifted by. It flapped in the warm breeze and swept over me, making my mouth water. I was starving! Maybe I could find a bakery.

We crossed the dusty street and passed a barber shop, an assayer's office, a clothing store. No bakery in sight.

As we stepped down to cross an alley, a short, fat man in a tight, green suit appeared. A red mark crossed his cheekbone and he wore a ratty, blue cap pulled down snug over his head. He made me uneasy, but I was so hungry I went up to him anyway.

"Say, mister, is there a place to eat around here?" I asked him.

The man's voice whistled through missing teeth as he spoke, "Ssstep over here, sssslow like."

I held back, suddenly afraid, but Tom nudged me forward.

"Better do like the man says, Jessie," he warned me. "He's got a gun."

Chapter 8

"A gun!" I gasped before Tom clamped his hand over my mouth. He steered me into the alley. Just up the street I heard more shouting and screaming.

In the alley another man appeared. This one stood tall and bony and needed a haircut. He wore a long, tan overcoat with patched elbows. His droopy eyes made him look like he hadn't slept in a month. From beneath his coat he pulled out a shotgun. I held my breath.

"They got a car?" the tall man asked the short man.

"I dunno," the short man answered.

"You *dummy!* You was supposed to get us a car."

The short man in green, aimed his pistol at Tom and asked, "Isss any of thesssssse carsssss yoursss, old man?"

With one quick glance at me, Tom replied, "Nope. Me and my granddaughter here were just out seeing the sights."

"What sssightss?" the short man whistled.

"What in tarnation?" squawked the tall man. I flinched at his barked words. He kicked a cloth bag at his feet. "First you give our driver the wrong directions and now you can't even come up with a getaway car."

Getaway car. Guns. Those screams up the street. All of a sudden I understood. These men were bank robbers!

"Aw, gimme another chanccce," whined the short man.

"You're more trouble than you're worth. Just what do you reckon we're to do with them?" He meant me and Tom.

The short man shrugged. "Tie 'em up, I guesssss."

"And let 'em identify us later?" the tall man asked. "We're gonna have to shoot 'em."

Shoot us! We had to get out of here. Hugging Victoria close, I thought quickly. Then I said, "Maybe we could help you find a car."

The men gazed at me. At first I grew hopeful. They'd let us go! Then the tall one's eyes narrowed.

"Just keep still, girl," he cracked. "I got heartaches enough as it is."

Heartaches? That gave me another idea, but I needed to act fast. Before these robbers decided to kill us!

I clutched the front of my overalls with one hand and cried out, "Oh, my heart!"

My eyelids fluttered. I crashed to the ground with Victoria still in my arms. I hoped Tom would think of the right thing to do.

"Oh, no, you've killed this dear child!" I heard Tom sob. "The poor thing had a bad heart."

"We didn't do it!" cried the short man. "It'sss not our fault!"

"What a rotten day," croaked the tall man. "To be sidekicked with the dumbest man alive. She's no deader than I am. This is a stupid trick."

There was no fooling him, but I kept my eyes closed tight anyway. I hoped they would just give up on us and go away.

Someone came close. I felt my arm being plucked up.

I opened my eyes slightly. The short one stooped beside me.

"Ssssay," he called out. "I think thissss gal'ss ssstill alive!"

"What a miracle," the tall man sneered.

I clenched my eyes tightly and started to pray.

BOOM!

I jerked. An explosion roared in the alley. For a second I couldn't hear anything at all.

Tom!

My eyes flew open. The tall man and Tom were struggling over the shotgun, the barrel aimed at the sky.

The short man started toward them, but I grabbed hold of his foot and yanked it close. I bit down on his ankle as hard as I could.

He screamed as he stumbled and fell next to me. I rolled away from him and jumped to my feet. The short man sprawled on the ground, clutching his foot and whimpering. I raced to help Tom just as he knocked the other man down.

Phleet! Phleeeeet!

The sound of a whistle stopped me. Then—

Pow! Pow! Pow!

More gunshots!

"All right, you!" came a voice. "Hands in the air."

A police officer stood in the alley, his gun aimed.

Rescued!

Even though they lay on the ground, the two despera-
dos raised their arms.

"You two get your hands up too," the police officer
ordered.

He meant Tom and me! I glanced at Tom. He had a
fearful kind of look in his eye I'd never seen there before.
I waited, anxious for him to speak up and explain, but he
said nothing. I didn't understand his silence.

Pointing at the men on the ground, I blurted out,
"Here're your robbers. They were about to shoot us."

A crowd surged into the alley and stood behind the
police officer. The officer continued to aim his gun at the
four of us.

"Up with your hands, all of you," the officer demanded.
"We'll sort this out at the station."

Several folks in the crowd cried out, "The girl's right.
Those two men, the two on the ground, they robbed the
bank."

I pointed to the cloth bag.

"Look, the money bag," I said. I slowly picked it up and
handed it to the police officer. Tom remained still, a little
sheepish I thought.

"That young lady and the old man—they saved the
day!" shouted someone in the crowd.

The officer seemed to be sizing us up. Finally he told
us, "OK, you're free to leave." Then he stepped past us

and collected the two scalawags.

The short one complained as he hobbled past me, "That girl bit me sssomething awful. I'll probably get sssome terrible disssease now."

"Nothing that several years behind bars won't cure," I advised him.

"Come on, Jessie, let's get back to the truck," Tom said.

I picked up my bundle and glanced around. "Wait. Where's Victoria?"

In all the commotion my newfound pet had vanished.

I pushed through the crowd, my eyes searching every patch of ground for the baby armadillo.

"Oh, Tom, Tom, she's gone!" I cried. *"She's gone!"*

Then, I spotted her. She waddled out into the street, her head down.

"Victoria!" I called out. *"Victoria!"* But she was no dog. The cry of her name didn't get her attention.

Tom dashed after her. A truck barreled down the street right at the helpless creature. My throat went dry as I pictured Victoria squashed just like her mama. *No!* Then my heart skipped a beat as Tom scooped her up and jumped out of the path of the speeding truck.

I leaned back against the building, closing my eyes and breathing hard. Tom planted Victoria back in my arms. I looked at him with tears of gratitude in my eyes. What a remarkable man. So brave. And spry too. Maybe he truly was my guardian angel. For certain he was Victoria's. But why had he acted so strange around that police officer?

Why hadn't he spoken up? I couldn't help thinking he had plenty of secrets. Things I might never know.

"We better find Lavern," Tom said, peering down the street.

I nodded, but before we could set out a man in a dark-blue suit planted himself in front of us. He stood a head shorter than Tom. His determined, gray eyes narrowed on us. He had a tight, grim mouth and a broad chin. His sparse salt-and-pepper moustache didn't add much to his face.

"Are you the two that tangled with those bank robbers?" he asked in an excited, creaky voice.

I looked at Tom. He'd become quiet again.

"We are," I told the man.

Unexpectedly, the man grinned. His steel eyes softened and sparkled with tears! He threw both arms around us, sweeping us up into a three-person hug. He laughed.

"You saved the day!" he exclaimed. "You have saved the very day!"

Dust-covered Lavern appeared behind him. He seemed dirtier than ever. "What's going on?"

The overjoyed man glanced suspiciously at Lavern and asked, "You know these folks?" Probably he wondered about a man who looked so filthy.

Lavern nodded uncertainly.

"Your friends here foiled the plans of a couple of bank robbers. Those scoundrels would've made off with everything if it hadn't been for these two."

Lavern's face instantly took on that greedy look I'd come to know so well.

"Well, well," he said with the smile of a snake. "I'll bet there's a re-ward for such an act of heroism."

Ignoring Lavern, the man in the blue suit said, "Let me introduce myself. I'm Merriwether T. Bascomb, president of the First National Bank."

He held out his hand. Tom shook it, then I did. Lavern tried to shake it too, but Mr. Bascomb had already withdrawn his hand.

"You folks live here?" Mr. Bascomb asked.

"We're just passing through," Lavern told him. "On our way to California."

"I see. Well, you'll have to be my guests tonight. I'll put you up at the El Dorado Hotel, and you can join me for dinner."

Victoria poked out her head from under my arm. Maybe she considered herself a guest of this hospitality too.

"Listen, I'll tell you what," Mr. Bascomb said. "While you get your things, I'll make arrangements with the hotel. See it? Just up the street there. Then I'll come back in, say" — he glanced at his watch, a silver pocket-watch that made a pretty song when he snapped it open — "in an hour and take you folks out to dinner. How does that sound?"

He spoke to Tom, but Lavern moved in.

"That would be fine." Lavern put his arm around Mr. Bascomb and ushered him away, whispering.

When Mr. Bascomb hurried up the street toward the hotel, Lavern spun around and snapped his fingers. *"Aha!* Money in the bank. This Bascomb's gonna re-ward us like princes. Like *princes!"*

Chapter 9

Dinner that night was wonderful. The diner Mr. Bascomb took us to was decorated inside with all sorts of Indian stuff—colorful blankets, clay pots, baskets, beaded dolls, and lovely silver and turquoise jewelry. A picture of President Roosevelt hung on the wall behind the cash register.

I ate chicken-fried steak, mashed potatoes, pinto beans, hot-buttered sourdough biscuits, cherry pie, and milk. Except for the mashed potatoes, which were lumpy, it had been a long time since I'd eaten so fine a meal. It was hard to imagine that just down the street I'd seen a soup kitchen full of hungry people. In fact, I felt a little guilty having eaten so well.

I looked around the table.

All of us—Tom, me, and Lavern—looked clean and neat. I had had my first bath since leaving Liberal. I'd put on a clean shirt, socks, and underwear. I'd even washed my butchered hair. I truly felt like a brand-new person. Even Lavern had bathed. His face was red and splotchy where he'd scrubbed off layers of grime. Now instead of a dust and sweat odor, he smelled of soap and toilet water.

But the bath and fine dinner seemed only to have soured his mood. He squirmed in his chair and scowled at Mr. Bascomb, which I found truly embarrassing. The banker ignored him and talked happily about life in Gallup. Then Lavern interrupted him and said he was "looking for greener pastures in California" and needed money for the trip, which I found a rude remark.

For about the tenth time that night Mr. Bascomb said, "I don't know what I would've done if you two"—he meant Tom and me—"hadn't come along and nabbed those thieves."

"Then why don't you bless us with a re-ward," I heard Lavern mutter. I hoped Mr. Bascomb didn't hear this, but I kicked Lavern under the table just in case.

"*Ow!*" Lavern cried out. He looked suspiciously around the table, as if trying to figure out the culprit.

I quickly changed the subject. "What will happen to those men, Mr. Bascomb?"

The banker took a sip of coffee and replied, "They'll be tried, probably found guilty, and then spend a good stretch in prison."

"I hope they stick those men in jail and throw away the key," I said.

Tom looked startled, like he'd just sat on a bee.

"People who steal other people's money are vile," I declared. I recalled the hard-working folks I knew back home who earned barely enough for food and shelter. I imagined them losing what little they had to some thieves. "They deserve to be locked up forever."

Well, that shut everyone up! Mr. Bascomb took out his musical watch and consulted it.

Lavern sat up. His eyes narrowed on Mr. Bascomb like he expected something big to happen.

"Well, folks, I have a suggestion," the banker remarked, snapping his watch cover closed. "We have a fine little movie house up the street. Anyone interested in seeing a picture show? It's a cowboy picture, I believe."

"I'd like to see that picture," Tom declared, his eyes brightening. "I'm partial to cowboy movies."

Lavern grunted.

"Well, then, let me pay for dinner and we'll go," Mr. Bascomb said. He strolled over to a woman standing beside the cash register.

Leaning past me, Lavern hissed, "This is an insult. We risk our lives and he don't even use the word 're-ward.'"

"*We* didn't risk anything, Lavern," Tom countered. "Jessie and me squared off against those bank robbers. You just happened along in time for all the congratulatin'."

Lavern grunted again as Mr. Bascomb rejoined us.

"Well," he smiled, "how about that picture?"

"I've got better things to do," Lavern grumbled. "I'm going to bed." He got up and stalked off.

Watching him leave, Mr. Bascomb asked, "What's wrong with your friend?"

"That's just Lavern," Tom replied.

Outside the moving picture house Mr. Bascomb paid for our tickets. Then he tipped his hat.

"I'd best be going home. The missus'll be expecting me

and I've got just enough time"—he took out his watch and consulted it again—"to tuck my son in for the night. Again, I thank you both for your bravery."

He shook our hands. In the light from the theater behind us I again saw tears in this banker's eyes. Everything I'd heard about bankers faded away. Daddy had never spoken ill of them, but I'd heard plenty of grumbling about them in Oklahoma and Kansas. Folks described them as men who'd sooner take your house and your land as to look at you. Mr. Bascomb sure didn't fit that description. He'd been nothing but kind from the moment we met. He put us up in a fine hotel for the night. He treated us to a great dinner. And now a moving picture show. And all I'd done was bite a man on the ankle!

Tom and I went inside. Through the whole picture Tom kept pointing out how it wasn't very realistic. He'd say, "I never knew a cowboy who couldn't sing. Any decent trail boss'd always pick fellas with voices that could calm the herd." Then he would grumble, "No outfit could afford to keep on that many cowboys during winter. We always got laid off for four or five months and then were told to come back for spring roundup."

Interesting as I found this information, I couldn't follow the picture with all his interruptions. Finally, I whispered, "Tom, please hush. I can't keep the story straight."

Afterward, Tom apologized for ruining the picture for me, but I told him he hadn't. He suggested we sit on a bench and rest a spell. I didn't know what he meant since we hadn't done anything to rest up from, but I agreed.

The night was so lovely I didn't want to go in just yet.

A light shone down from the side of a building behind us. A few insects fluttered in our faces. Tom gazed at the stars twinkling above us and fiddled with something poking out of his boot heel. I watched people go in and come out of a still-opened trading post across the street.

"Jessie, you said some things at dinner that got me to thinking," Tom said. He stroked his moustache.

I looked at him. "What things?"

"About how those bank robbers oughta be locked up forever. That was pretty hard talk."

"It's just the way I feel," I told him.

"What if I was to tell you that I . . ." he began. His eyes darted away from me. I thought of how he had behaved around that police officer just a few hours ago.

"You what?" I asked. I got a nervous feeling that I was about to find out something I'd rather not know.

He frowned at me, frowned at the stars. "This trip Lavern and me are on. There's no gold mine."

I'd had my suspicions about the mine, but a chill worked its way up my back. I didn't say anything.

"Truth is, we're after some loot all right but not in a mine," he said. "It's money that got stole years ago."

"*Stolen* money?" The news took me by surprise.

He nodded and swatted at the insects in front of his face. When he returned his hands to his lap, I noticed they were shaking. "It's hid in this town called Harvest-of-Gold, California. Not far from where you're headed."

"Stolen from where?"

"A bank, back in 1889. The bank's probably gone. I reckon most or all of the people the money belonged to are dead by now."

"How'd you know about the robbery? And where the loot is hid?"

Tom sat very still, looking into my eyes. His own eyes were dark and bright against his pale face. I grew nervous, like I couldn't take a breath until he answered my question.

"I helped steal it."

His words exploded in my head. *Steal?* He was joshing me, surely. But the look on his face told me otherwise.

No! This couldn't be.

Suddenly I felt scared and alone. Like I didn't know this man at all. Could it be true that he had once robbed a bank? Only a few hours ago I considered him my guardian angel. I shook my head.

"Jessie, in 1893, I got shot trying to rob another bank in Colorado. They caught me and after the trial they stuck me away. It was almost like what you said at dinner. Like they threw away the key. I lost track of the years myself. I was thirty-two when I went to prison and seventy-four when I got out. Almost three months ago."

I just gazed at him, dumbfounded.

"You'd better close your mouth because I've eaten bugs before. They ain't that good."

"But—but—" I didn't know what to say or what to think. Here I sat, an ex-convict at my side. I'd been traveling with him lo these many miles.

"Probably I should've told you about my past earlier," he confessed. "But it ain't easy to talk about."

My mind raced back to finding the gun in the back of the pickup that first day. I had to know something. "Did you ever ... *kill* anybody?"

He shook his head and answered, "No, Jessie. Sure, I carried a gun and pointed it at folks, but I can at least say that I never used it. I was no Jesse James or Bob Dalton. The only thing special about me was the name the newspapers stuck me with. When they found out my name and that I was born in Tennessee, they started calling me 'Tennessee Tom.'"

So that's what "Tennessee Tom" meant. An outlaw nickname! All sorts of thoughts pounded in my brain. I felt like I was sitting on that bench by myself. Now so many things made sense: Tom's nervousness around the police officer when we'd caught the bank robbers; Lavern's teasing Tom about Billy the Kid and riding the outlaw trail; and the years since Tom had last seen his wife and daughter.

"I'm sure you're ashamed now to be in my company," Tom went on. "But maybe you can see fit to forgive me for not being straight with you from the start."

Anger exploded inside me. I yelled at him, "*Forgive!* You're *still* a robber! Except this time you aim to steal money that's already been stolen once."

"I'm not keeping the loot, Jessie. That's the truth. I'm going to turn it over to the authorities. Lavern thinks we're splitting it, but I'll straighten him out."

Tom was right. I did feel ashamed of him. When I'd
thought he was just a cowboy, he was kind of a hero to
me. A guardian angel even. But now, but now. . . .

"People can change, Jessie. When you said in the diner
they oughta put those men in prison forever, you forgot
that some of them'll come to see the error of their ways.
That don't make what they did right. But the Lord for-
gives and forgets, so we oughta at least give folks a
chance."

My anger burned. I couldn't even look this old convict
in the eye. So what if he was sorry now for his outlaw
ways. He had *lied* to me!

I jumped up from the bench and shouted at him,
"You're a *liar!* All that about returning the money. It's—
it's lies! No wonder you haven't seen your daughter in all
this time. She probably *hates* you!"

I turned and ran all the way back to the hotel. Tears
flew from my face. As I ran, I thought of Mama and Daddy
and all the tears I'd cried when they had left me with
Aunt Edna. And now Tom. He had betrayed me too.

I hated him! I hated him!

Tom's calling after me sounded like a tiny voice in the
dark.

Chapter 10

I slept poorly, my mind filled with the awful truths I'd found out. How could I keep traveling with an ex-convict? Even worse, a lying ex-convict? A bitter taste filled my mouth all night and no amount of water could wash it out. I'd never be able to forgive him. I buried my head in my pillow and tried to sleep, but I kept seeing Tom's face and hearing his terrible words.

During the night I took out my Bible and on a blank end page I wrote *T* and drew a short black mark underneath it.

It seemed people were always disappointing me.

When the morning sun peeked through the curtains one thought was in my mind. *I had only three days to get to California.*

I didn't have much choice. Whatever Tom had done, I needed this ride. Lavern wasn't likely to let me come along any farther without paying, so I climbed from bed, dressed, and stuck my remaining two dollars into my overalls pocket. Then I went down the hall and rapped at his door.

He opened it faster than I expected.

Sizing me up with his usual unpleasant expression, he said, "What do *you* want?"

I looked him in the eye and said, "A ride. I still need to get to San Bernardino."

"Why should I take you even one more mile?" he sneered. Sleep had done nothing to improve the man's mood. "You owe me for the ride you got yesterday."

He was right. I reached into my pocket and dug out the dollar I had promised him. He snatched it from me before I could even hand it over.

"I'm prepared to pay for any ride you give me," I told him.

"Yeah? How much?" His black eyes gleamed behind his spectacles. I saw greed there. And love of money.

"All that I have," I told him. "I've got enough to buy a train ticket, but it'd be better if I could just ride with you." I didn't figure I was lying. A dollar ought to buy a train ticket to somewhere.

As usual, his hand shot out. "Pay now," he said.

I shook my head. "I'm twelve years old, Mr. Brewster, but I'm no simpleton. I'll pay you at the end of the ride. My daddy'll probably be able to give you a little extra as well." Not much extra, though, I thought.

He considered my offer. I knew the idea of getting a bonus from Daddy appealed to him. Finally, he took off his eyeglasses and tried to wipe them on his shirttail. They fell apart again.

"Drat!" he spat. "Listen here, girlie. We're pulling out of here by 8 o'clock. If you're late, you're left."

Then he slammed his door shut. I sighed in relief.

An hour later the three of us, along with Victoria and Juniper, climbed into the dusty pickup. Tom wore a sheepish look on his face, but I just looked away. I kept thinking, *you can travel with them. Just don't have anything else to do with them.*

Mr. Bascomb stopped by to thank us again, and then we headed out, leaving Gallup and continuing west.

As the scenery whizzed past, I thought about the things Tom had told me last night. They still seemed so hard to believe. At my feet, Victoria scratched around in the box I'd found for her. I reached down and patted her spiny back. She appeared happy nibbling on the few bugs I'd come across in the weeds behind the hotel.

I looked out the window and watched New Mexico end and Arizona begin. The rugged land stretched out for miles, covered with flat-topped rocky hills, cactus, and grayish-green brush.

"I'm grateful for the possibility of rain," Tom said, "but I don't like the looks of those clouds."

He pointed at some black clouds far off to the west. Their color reminded me of last month when we got the worst blow ever in Liberal. I remembered Black Sunday when the afternoon sky got dark as night. Sand and grit hailed against the doors and windows. All the Tyler kids, even Walter, cried. Even then Aunt Edna had spanked me—for not trying hard enough to keep her kids away from the windows. She had been plenty scared herself.

We met a few wet cars headed east, their windshield

wipers swishing, their lights on. A couple of them flashed their lights and honked their horns at us. What did that mean? Other cars whizzed past, going west, plunging headlong into the darkness ahead.

Just as we reached the dark clouds, the rain hit with a fury. It came all at once, not little by little. Lavern grumbled and switched on the wipers. Only the one on his side worked. It scraped and squealed against the glass something awful. Ahead, I saw lightning flash. It zig-zagged down to earth like a crooked snake. When, seconds later, thunder exploded in the sky, I jumped.

I tried to peer through the hammering rain. All I could make out were waves of water streaming across the windshield. Lavern hunched over the wheel, staring into the storm. I worried that he wouldn't be able to keep the pickup on the road.

"Better pull over till this lets up some," Tom advised.

"We gotta get through this," growled Lavern.

"Looks like there ain't no end to it. Besides, the road might start flooding out. It ain't even paved here."

Inside the truck's cab it sounded like a hundred hammers smashing the roof. The pounding scared me so badly I shut my eyes, covered my ears with my hands, and sang:

> When I draw this fleeting breath
> When mine eyelids close in death,
> When I soar to worlds unknown,
> See Thee on Thy judgment throne,

Rock of Ages cleft for me,
Let me hide myself in Thee.

It didn't cheer me to sing about death, but I clung to
the words "when I soar to worlds unknown." I wished
then that I could fly away. Far away. For a moment I
forgot all about finding Mama and Daddy in California. I
just wanted to soar high above this terrible, terrible
storm.

Unexpectedly, my side of the pickup plunged down.
Then my body slammed against the door.

Dear Lord, what was happening?

"*Whoaaaaaa!*" cried Lavern.

"Turn her back!" Tom ordered as he grabbed the dash-
board and leaned toward Lavern, struggling to keep from
falling on top of me.

"*I'm trying! I'm trying!*"

"Try harder, Lavern!"

Lavern yanked the steering wheel, but it did no good.
The pickup stopped moving forward. Instead, it slid sideways. I jerked around trying to find something to hold
onto. I braced my feet against the door, leaning back toward Tom. He leaned toward Lavern. I heard Victoria
scuttling around in the box on the floor. I was breathing
pretty hard.

We slid to a stop.

"It's over," Lavern said.

"What happened?" I asked.

"Truck washed off the road," Tom replied. "We're on

the edge of an arroyo."

"A what?"

"A dry creek bed."

I fumbled with the window crank. When I got the window open a crack, a blast of water hit me in the face. Through the downpour I made out something. It wasn't dry though. It looked more like a raging river. The pickup was perched on the very edge!

"Shut that window, girlie, before you flood us out!" cried Lavern.

I cranked the window up. "We're about to be washed into a river!"

Just then the pickup jolted sideways again. Lavern and Tom fell against me, crushing me against the door.

The pickup skidded once more. Then a pause. No one spoke. I gasped for air and thought I could hear Tom's heart pounding. I knew I could hear my own.

Then the pickup buckled and rolled over. We crashed against the side. *Ouch!* Then the roof. *Blam!* The pickup kept turning, the three of us rolling around together in the seat, our arms and legs bashing against each other. I clenched the door handle with both hands. Somehow we ended right side up again.

"Oww! I think my arm's broke," Lavern whined as he and Tom untangled.

Ignoring him, Tom said, "Jessie, you OK?"

I nodded, even though I did feel sick to my stomach, like I'd just gotten off a wild horse.

I bent down to check on Victoria. I couldn't believe it.

She was still in her box and seemed fine.

Tom nudged Lavern and said, "See if the truck starts."

Lavern groaned, holding his arm. He tried the engine. Nothing.

"We've gotta get outta here," declared Tom. "Grab what you can and let's go."

Lavern dug beneath his seat. "Where is it? Where is it?" he cried.

"Lavern, *go!*" Tom yelled.

Finally, Lavern yanked a burlap bag from beneath the seat. He shoved open his door and plunged out.

"It's two feet deep out here!" he called back to us.

Tom followed, taking nothing with him.

I scooped up the box with Victoria. I set my Bible and my doll Marjorie in with her. Then I spread the empty pillowcase over the box.

"Hurry, the truck's about to break away," Tom called.

I didn't understand till I scrambled outside. Rain hit me like a thousand icy needles, stinging my face and arms. I shivered as the freezing floodwater surged up to my knees. Blinking through the downpour, I gasped as I saw the pickup perched on a mound of mud. The water in the arroyo rushed by so fast that the pickup rocked from side to side.

The river swelled. Tom grabbed me and tore me away from the truck just as it broke free and sailed away.

"Wait!" Lavern cried out. *"Juniper!"*

He'd been so determined to find the burlap bag that he'd forgotten to save his pet. I watched the pickup vanish in the downpour. The poor critter. She'd been a good traveling companion, as good as Victoria.

"She'll be all right," Tom declared. "She'll just be downstream a ways is all."

We kept backing up as the water rose. Soon it had us backed up all the way to the steep sides of the arroyo. Tom pointed up. Through the rain I saw what he meant. We'd have to climb to escape. And we'd have to start climbing soon or we'd end up downstream like Juniper, only without a vehicle to carry us in.

As if afraid he'd miss his chance, Lavern tied his bag to his belt and lunged against the cliff. Wildly, he threw his arms and legs into the effort, grabbing at every clump of rock and mud. He'd make it up a few feet, then break loose and slide back down.

The chilly water kept rising.

Shielding his eyes, Tom sized up the side of the arroyo as if deciding which route to take. Finally, he stretched up and dug his hand into what looked like a clump of red mud. He pulled himself up. He then kicked the toes of his green boots into the earth, getting a firm foothold. *Hurrah!* Little by little, he worked his way up the cliff.

"That ornery old coot's left me behind!" fumed Lavern.

I started to follow Tom, using the holes he'd made, trying to juggle the box with Victoria and my things.

Tom yelled down, "Come on, Jessie, get just a little way up and then grab hold."

He dangled his black coat over the side of the cliff like a rope. "Go up the way I did."

"Outta my way, *scamp!*" Lavern hollered.

He threw me aside and followed Tom's route up to the coat. The frantic way he tore at the earth made the hand and toe holds crumble and fall away.

I watched as Tom tugged his blood kin the rest of the way up. Even through the thunderous crashing rain I could hear Tom shouting at Lavern for coming up first.

"Jessie, *leave the box!*" yelled Tom. "Come on. *Quick!* The water's rising fast."

The icy water splashed above my knees. How long before this arroyo filled up? *Lord, Lord, help me now!*

Chapter 11

I knew I had to give up the box. But what about Victoria? Could armadillos swim? I didn't rescue her just to let her drown in a muddy river.

The water rose fast. Already it surged around my waist. I plucked Victoria from the box. She rolled into a tight, little ball. I wedged her and my Bible under the bib of my overalls.

I had to drop the box. That meant giving up Marjorie and my magazine pictures. The pictures could be replaced. But there'd never be another Marjorie. She was the only doll I'd ever had. I tried desperately to hang onto her too, but it was no use. I just had to give her up.

Hot tears streaked down my cheeks. "Marjorie, I'm sorry," I sobbed. "I hope some little girl finds you and takes good care of you." I let go of the box. It sailed downstream. I felt like following it.

"Hurry, Jessie!" Tom called out.

The water pulled at me as if it wanted to carry me downstream after Marjorie. I stretched up, straining to grab hold of the side of the arroyo. It came apart in my hand. I gasped and tried again. And again. Every handful of earth turned into a handful of mud.

"Dig out pockets and climb up!" Tom yelled down to me.

"I'm trying!" I yelled back.

I shivered and the water kept tugging at me, urging me to give up and let go. I saw myself floating downstream, maybe even catching up with Marjorie. Part of me wanted just to let go and be carried away. Then I thought, *I have to get up this arroyo! I still have a long trip ahead of me. I'd saved Victoria. Now I need to save myself!*

"Climb, Jessie!" Tom screamed.

I looked up. Tom's coat hung a few feet above me. If only I could reach it! With rain stinging my face, I blindly stretched up again.

Just then my fingers grasped something hard. It felt like a stiff rope. I gripped hard and tugged.

It held fast!

With all my strength, I pulled myself up. My feet scrambled for toeholds. I found one that held just long enough for me to push up again. My hands followed the rope-like thing. A root—that's what it was! I pulled up again. Tom's coat dangled above my head. I reached out. My fingertips touched it. Then I shoved myself up as hard as I could. I caught hold of the coat!

"Thatagirl!" Tom's voice sang down to me.

I held on tight and felt myself being pulled up. I tried to push up with my legs, but I felt so tired. My arms grew weak. I wanted to let go. *Don't let go, Jessie,* I told myself. *Hang on!* Shutting my eyes, I started to pray. Then I felt a hand grip mine. Another hand came around me, yanking me hard. The next thing I knew I lay stretched out on the mud at the edge of the cliff. Rain splattered in my face and Tom knelt beside me, breathing hard.

I felt a wiggle under my overall's bib. Victoria! She stuck her nose out and sniffed.

Tom gasped, "Come on, Jessie. Let's find us some shelter."

Exhausted, I tramped across the soggy ground beside him. With each step I felt the mud sucking at my shoes. Twice I nearly lost them. I grabbed hold of Tom's arm and clung to it as I tried to keep up with his long strides. My clothes felt like a soaked second skin.

I started shivering and couldn't stop.

"There's Lavern," Tom yelled. "He's found a place."

Moments later we reached an old building. Lavern stood in the doorway. We hurried inside. *Dry!*

I collapsed and huddled against a crumbling adobe wall. Beneath me was a dirt floor. I pulled Victoria and my waterlogged Bible out of my overalls and set them beside me. Gripping my legs, I sat there shivering. My teeth chattered and I hugged my arms around my chest, trying to get warm.

Beside the door Tom and Lavern rummaged through a pile of trash they'd found. Tin cans clattered and glass broke as they flung the stuff around.

Tom said, "Look, dry matches—and candles!"

I heard wood cracking. Although cold, wet, and exhausted, I forced myself to get up and go over to them.

"Jessie, here, tear up this paper," Tom instructed, handing me several large, poster-like sheets. "We've got to build a fire or we'll all end up with pneumonia."

I tore the musty paper and tossed the pieces in a pile. Tom struck a match and it lit right up! He dropped it onto the paper and soon we had a smoky fire going.

"Find more wood," said Tom. "I've got to take care of this smoke or we'll run outta breathing air."

The light from the fire helped me see inside the building. Four windows were covered with ragged, dusty curtains. On one of the seeping walls I spotted a picture. I walked over to it. The picture was small and it showed Jesus sitting with children all around Him. I looked around. At the other end of the building I noticed a tall, narrow box. Behind the box stood a table. Above the table hung a cross made from rough timber.

"A *church!*" I exclaimed. "This is a church."

"It certainly is," Tom answered from a corner. He ripped down the dusty curtains and broke out the windows. Almost at once the smoke in the place cleared out.

I lit the candles Tom had found and set them around the small room.

Lavern reached for the cross hanging on the wall. I couldn't believe what he was doing.

"Don't touch it!" I screamed.

He jumped. "Don't yell at me, girlie! I got the shakes bad enough as it is." He turned back to the cross.

"Stop!" I cried. "You can't burn *that!*"

Tom came over to me. "Jessie's right, Lavern. Leave

the cross where it is."

"It's wood, ain't it?"

"Leave it be."

Lavern snapped, "I'm sick and tired of you ordering me around. You may have this girlie here fooled into thinking you're some kinda hero, but you don't fool me none. Truth is, you're nothing but a broke down, old ex-con."

As troubled as I was about Tom's past, I didn't care for Lavern's remark.

"You don't know a bit about what I'm thinking," I told him. "People change. They can get better if they're close to the Lord." I spoke the words, but I didn't really believe what I was saying.

"Ha!" laughed Lavern. "He's about as close to the Lord as Jesse James."

Tom gazed at me in that smoky, empty old church. I saw in his eyes the something I had seen so many days ago in Liberal. A kindness. A warmth. A spark of faith.

I wanted to go to him and throw my arms around him. But I just couldn't forgive him. I kept remembering his lying to me. I went over to the stack of wood, lifted up a piece of broken chair, and tossed it into the fire.

Lavern seemed to remember the burlap bag tied to his belt. He pulled it free and dumped the contents onto the floor. The gun I'd discovered in the back of the pickup dropped to the dirt floor.

"What!" he cried out. "Where's. . . ."

He tore the bag open, ripping it apart as if searching desperately for something.

"My money!" he moaned. "Where's my money?"

"You must of grabbed the wrong bag," Tom said.

At once, Lavern swooped down and plucked up the pistol. He waved it at Tom.

"This's *your* doing, old man!" he shouted. The sound of his voice echoed in the old church and seemed to make the walls shake. "It's all your fault!"

"You grabbed the bag, Lavern, not me. Put that gun down before you make me mad."

"But you rushed me! Thanks to you, all my money's gone. And Juniper too."

"You couldn't of had that much money."

"What do you know?" Lavern argued. He lowered the gun a bit. "I had nearly a hundred dollars. *A hundred!*" He raised the gun at Tom and cocked the hammer back. "I oughta kill you, you worthless old coot!"

I stepped back. Tom reached out and knocked the gun from his grasp. An explosion rocked the inside of the church. I flinched as dust and adobe dropped on our heads from the bullet striking the ceiling. A wisp of smoke drifted up from the floor where the pistol lay. I kicked it to Tom.

"You fool," Tom told Lavern, retrieving the gun. "I've had my fill of your greed. From now on, you're on your own. When I find that bank loot, I'm turning it over to the authorities. You get nothing. You hear that, Lavern? *Nothing.*"

Tom unloaded the pistol and stuffed the bullets in his pants pocket.

"Ha!" barked Lavern. "You want to keep that loot all for yourself. You're just putting on an act for this kid."

"I guess you'll see for yourself."

Tom turned to me and said, "You'd better get out of those wet clothes and try to dry out."

He shook the dust from some curtains and draped them over me. The dust and the musty smell made me start coughing.

Tom took off his drenched black coat and purple shirt and pulled off his undershirt. His chest looked pale and sunken, reminding me of all those years he'd spent behind bars. He used a knife to cut up his undershirt into long narrow strips and tied them together to make a rope. One end of the homemade rope he tied to a nail in the wall and the other he tied to the tall narrow box. Then he began to drape wet clothes over the rope.

"I'm giving you some privacy," he told me with a wink.

Holding the curtains around me, I took off my shoes and socks and laid them by the fire to dry. Then I stripped down to my wet drawers. I wrung out my cold, drippy overalls and shirt, and hung them over the rope. I huddled cold and shivering beneath the curtains, even though the fire had begun to warm the room. I heard someone break up another chair and throw the pieces on the fire. No one spoke.

After a while I squatted on the dirt floor beside Victoria. She had curled back into a ball and seemed to be sleeping. By the light of a nearby candle I opened my Bible. The pages stuck together, all soggy from the rain

and the flood. I fanned the pages as best I could and laid
the book down to dry. I came to the page full of black
marks and recalled why they were there. It seemed a
hundred years ago that I'd been living with Aunt Edna
and her family. Years since I'd last been spanked.

Mean as she was, Aunt Edna's face in my mind started
me crying. I just broke down like a big baby and couldn't
stop. I sobbed like that for a long time.

Getting to California seemed impossible now. Time was
running out.

Chapter 12

I stayed awake all night. Shivering on the packed earth floor, I could barely remember what had taken place the night before.

I heard Tom and Lavern breathing, but that was all. The roar of rain hammering the roof and the crack of thunder in the distance were gone.

I pushed off the dusty curtain covering me and got to my feet. My muslin drawers were still plenty wet. Cold and trembling, I felt my clothes hanging from Tom's homemade rope. Still damp. I fished out Mama's letter from my overalls pocket. My remaining dollar, wadded and soggy, dropped to the floor. All the writing on the letter had washed off, like the paper had never been written on to begin with. I stood there for the longest time, wiping at the tears in my eyes. Finally, I crumpled the page into a ball and threw it, hard, on the ground.

Peeking over the curtain of clothes, I saw Tom and Lavern sleeping, Lavern still in his wet clothes and Tom under several layers of yellowed newspapers. Tom's green boots, caked with mud, lay nearby. I remembered something about them—something protruding from a boot heel. I reached for the boots and examined each heel.

It was the right boot. I found Tom's pocket knife on the floor and scraped away the dried mud. Then I pried at the heel. It took some doing.

Finally, I worked the heel loose enough to pull out the object wedged inside.

It was a piece of white paper, folded many times. Opening it, I saw a drawing done with a careful hand in black ink. I didn't understand the drawing or the writing except for the arrows showing north and south. I did know, though, that it was a map. I folded it in half, tucked it away in my soaked Bible, and closed the gap in the heel. Then I returned the boots and the knife.

Victoria scurried over by the table. It occurred to me that she hadn't eaten in a while. The poor thing was probably starving.

I hid the money back in my Bible and put on my cold, damp clothes. Still shivering, I started coughing so bad I had to sit on the floor and wait it out. *Whew!*

The men continued to sleep. I picked up Victoria and crept past them to the door. As bad as I felt, Arizona looked beautiful. The brown earth seemed cleaner somehow after all the rain. Above, clouds were streaked purple and red from the rising sun. I shut my eyes and breathed the fresh morning air.

I grew very cold and started shaking. Opening my eyes, I saw what really surrounded me.

Miles and miles of nothing. We had lost the pickup and

our food. This truly did look like the middle of nowhere.

I'd left Liberal on Saturday, four long days ago. That meant I had only two days to get to California. And no ride. No food. No water. *What was I going to do?*

"That blasted rain finally stop?"

Lavern's voice broke into my thoughts.

I turned around and saw him standing behind me, smelling like a wet dog. He truly looked like a man slapped down by hard times. At that moment I pitied him, in spite of his disagreeable ways. As bad as I felt, I wanted to say something to cheer him up.

"I'm sorry about Juniper," I told him. "I know what it's like to lose a pet. I had a cat when we lived on a farm. Mister Boots. But he got distemper and—"

"I *hate* cats," Lavern spat, interrupting me.

What a spiteful man!

"Is there nothing you *do* like?" I snapped back.

Scowling at me, he tore off his eyeglasses. He tried cleaning them on his shirttail. As usual, they fell apart.

"Drat! Yes, girlie, there's plenty of things I like. I like having a reliable car. I like sleeping under my own roof. I like having enough money so I don't have to worry about my next meal. I like peace and quiet, none of which I've enjoyed since you stowed away on this trip."

"Don't start in on her again," Tom said. He had gotten up and dressed. He wore his boots. He rubbed the back of his neck and gazed past me at the rugged hills. His purple shirt hung wrinkled and damp on him. In the morning light he looked thin and pale, like he had plain worn down.

But he shot me a warm smile and said, "Don't worry, Jessie, we'll make it to California one way or another."

Lavern's voice crackled through the still morning air. "Yeah? Well, just how do we get outta here?"

Tom shrugged. "I reckon we walk till we come across some folks."

"And eat what? There's nothing out here but lizards and snakes and this little poor man's pig."

He meant Victoria. I leaped between the armadillo and Lavern. "She's a good pet and she's no trouble."

"Just like *you're* no trouble?" Lavern said.

I plucked Victoria from the ground where she was hunting for bugs and held her in my arms.

Lavern stalked off.

Tom called out, "Where do you think you're going?"

Lavern stopped but didn't turn around. He yelled, "If you have to know, I'm gonna follow that blasted river. Maybe I can find the pickup and my valuables if anything's left."

Tom shook his head and went back into the church. I watched Lavern trudge off toward the arroyo. Moments later Tom came out loading the pistol. Hugging Victoria, I stepped back.

His eyes latched onto me. "I guess you still think me pretty much a scoundrel, for lying to you and all."

"I don't think that at all," I answered, though I didn't sound too convincing, even to myself. Somehow, I just couldn't bring myself to forgive him.

"Maybe not, but I can see you don't think much of me."

He disappeared around the corner of the church.

I sat in the doorway and watched Victoria as she nibbled on a black beetle she had sniffed out. Thinking about California and how far I still had to travel, I felt foolish for just sitting around waiting as if I expected a bird or, better yet, an angel to swoop down from the sky and carry me off.

Pow! Pow! I flinched at the sound of the shots. A few minutes later Tom appeared. He held up a large lizard, its head a bloody stump. I moved out of his way.

"Breakfast!" he announced.

"You're going to *eat* that?" I asked, disgusted.

"Lizards are edible," he said. "Roasted just right they don't taste too bad."

I felt nearly faint with hunger and weariness from no sleep, but the thought of eating a lizard made me sick.

Tom sat down at the campfire in the church and started skinning that lizard. I couldn't watch. I returned to my place in the doorway, my back to him, and kept an eye on Victoria.

I heard Tom breaking up another chair and stoking the fire. Soon the flames warmed my back. They felt good. Off in the distance I saw Lavern stalking back, kicking at clumps of rock. When I caught the first whiff of that lizard cooking, I got up and went over to Victoria.

Then I heard it. A strange noise. *Ka-chunk ka-chunk ka-chunk.* The sound was distant but growing nearer.

Off a ways I spotted the dark shape of a vehicle. A car! We would be rescued!

I jumped up and waved my arms. Lavern, who had just gotten back, turned and looked.

"Hey!" he cried out.

The car rumbled over the terrible rutted road, bouncing high and slamming down hard. It was a boxy, rattletrap-looking machine, black but with much of its paint worn away and badly banged up. Dried red paint drops trickled down from the roof. The car skidded to a stop, throwing up mud and grit at Lavern who stood in its path. It was a foolish place to locate yourself, smack dab in the middle of a road with a vehicle approaching. You never knew the condition of a person's brakes.

For a moment Lavern and the driver behind the mud-splattered windshield seemed to stare at each other like a pair of stubborn enemies aching for a fight.

Lavern kicked at a wad of tumbleweed wedged between the front bumper and the grill. The car door swung open.

"I hope you ain't damaging my vehicle," came a raspy voice from inside the car.

Lavern straightened abruptly, as if preparing himself for trouble.

Out of the car climbed a woman wearing a red flannel shirt with big holes in the elbows. Her jeans were caked with mud and tied at the waist with a rope belt. She wore high-topped boots, like I'd seen on the pilot Charles Lindbergh in the newsreels. Thick curls of black hair stuck out from beneath an aviator's helmet, the goggles around her neck like a weird necklace. Red lipstick streaked

across her wide mouth. In her right hand she gripped a
shotgun.

Lavern's mouth gaped open in shock. It seemed clear
he'd never run into anyone quite like this lady before. I
hadn't either.

"The name's Hazel Womack," the woman called out
with her harsh voice. "I didn't expect to find many live
folks around here after last night's storm."

Tom stood in the doorway with his half-cooked lizard
on a stick. He set it aside and came over to the car.

"We didn't expect to see anyone at all," he declared.
"We got caught in a flooded arroyo and managed to hike
over here for the night. The pickup washed away on us."

"I saw it, turned over on its side," the woman said. "A
real mess. I feared an untimely end for its passengers."

"You *saw* it?" gasped Lavern. He moved toward her.
"Where is it? Take me over there! I gotta get . . . something I left it in."

"You're outta luck, mister," Hazel Womack said. "A
whole flock of folks are going over it. There's a lot of
people out of work in a town near here. I guess they—"

"*Thieves!*" cried Lavern. "Dirty rotten thieves! They
stole my money. All I had!"

He sank to the ground, sitting right in the middle of a
mud puddle.

Hazel Womack's thick black eyebrows shot up at the
spectacle of Lavern.

Then she turned her attention back to Tom and me.
"Well, come on, cowboys and cowgirls. Hop in. You're

welcome to ride along with me. I'm headed back to Flagstaff. I don't like digging in the mud."

I didn't know what she meant by "digging in the mud," but I didn't ask. I went back into the church, grabbed my Bible, came out, and scooped Victoria from the ground.

As I climbed into the front seat beside the woman, I said, "I hope you don't have bad feelings about armadillos."

She looked at me, then reached over and patted Victoria's armor. My pet rolled up into a tight ball.

"I like all critters except rattlesnakes and Gila monsters."

Before anyone else could utter a word we rumbled off toward Flagstaff, Arizona.

"I've been digging out so much of Arizona, I've probably lowered the sea level a thousand feet," Hazel declared. She liked all the car windows down, even though the breeze blew cold. I felt chilled to the bone, what with the cold air and damp clothes, but I didn't want to complain since she'd been so kind to rescue us.

"What do you mean by 'digging'?" Tom asked her.

She settled herself behind the wheel. "I'm a kind of amateur archeologist. I dig up bones, arrowheads, pots, old Spanish stirrups. Junk nobody'd want except museums and folks like me who are crazy about the past."

For some reason I thought about Tom and his past. His distant outlaw past and his prison past. And the past that included a daughter who'd grown up without him.

"Was that a snake I saw you cooking?" Hazel asked.

Tom called out from the back seat, "Lizard. We lost all our grub in the flood."

"There's a paper sack back there on the floor," Hazel said. Help yourself to the bread and some of that beef jerky in the jar."

Lavern grabbed the sack and snatched out a loaf of bread. He ripped off half the loaf and began stuffing it into his mouth. Tom took the other half and tore off smaller pieces for me and him. The rest he put back into the sack. Then he wrestled the jar from Lavern, opened it, and handed me a piece of beef jerky. I went after it, but it was so tough to chew that I gave up and ate the bread.

"The beef jerky's plenty tough," Hazel told us. "It was given to me by a sheriff who said he was planning to use it to make a pair of chaps."

Tom laughed. "It's too tough for that."

I started laughing too, but I fell into another coughing fit. This time I coughed so hard I could hardly get my breath. My whole body shook, until I plumb wore out.

Hazel reached over and felt my head. "This girl's feverish and near exhausted."

She rolled up her window and told Tom and Lavern to do the same. The last thing I remembered was Tom wrapping a dusty old blanket around me as I slumped down in the front seat. Then I slept.

Chapter 13

After that everything was a blur. I caught a glimpse of the outside of some enormous two-story house. People kept leaning over me—Hazel, Tom, then someone I didn't know. Lavern kept out of it. I think Hazel gave me a hot bath. I remembered soaking in water. Then everyone left me alone in a strange bed in a strange bedroom. When I drifted off again, I don't think anything could have awakened me.

When I finally did wake up, I didn't know where I was.

I leaned on one elbow and looked around. My narrow bed occupied a small room with a sloped ceiling. Light streamed in the one small window, making a warm yellow rectangle on the polished wood floor. Beside the bed stood a round wicker table. On it lay my Bible and a tray with a glass of milk, toast, and a bowl of some kind of soup, steam still rising from it. One straight-backed chair sat opposite the bed. Laid across the chair were my overalls and shirt. They were clean and starched and ironed. My shoes and clean socks lay next to the chair.

Someone had even polished my shoes. Tom.

Everything in the room, including me, smelled so clean.

Beside the bed was a small wooden crate with Victoria in it. She nibbled on something someone had put in there.

"Have we both died and gone to heaven?" I asked her.

I heard voices outside the door. After a bit the door opened quietly. In tiptoed Tom. Behind him was Hazel and a bald-headed man I'd never seen before.

Tom's dark eyes brightened. "Jessie, you're awake! This here's Henry, Hazel's brother." He nodded to the bald man. "He took right away to little Victoria. Got that crate for her and dug up some worms."

"Nice to meet you, Sir," I said with a faint voice. "Thank you for your kindness." I had just noticed I was wearing a man's cotton undershirt for a gown. I guessed the shirt to be Henry's.

"We've been waiting for you to wake up," Tom continued. "We thought you might sleep through the rest of 1935."

I gasped at what he said. *"Wha*—How long have I slept?"

"Since we got here yesterday," Tom answered.

"Then this is—*Thursday?*" I cried. "Oh, no, I've lost a whole day! What time is it?"

Tom sat on the edge of the bed. I searched his face for a trace of worry, but he just smiled at me.

"It's about 5 o'clock in the afternoon. But don't you fret, missy. Hazel here knows all about your troubles. She's got a plan for getting you to California in time."

"That's right," Hazel said with her raspy voice. "Heaven knows I understand all about a child wishing to be with her parents. That's for sure. Me and Henry are orphans, left in a basket as babes right outside a big orphanage in Denver. Never could get over wondering who my real parents were, but we never found them. Anyway, young lady, I'm gonna fly you to San Bernardino. We can leave at first light tomorrow morning."

"*Fly?*" I asked. "You mean in an airplane?"

"She's a pilot!" Tom exclaimed.

"That's right. I got me a little red Waco. It's a beaut. Two seats up front and one in back. You'll get a little wind and radiator water in your face, but I can get you there in a couple of hours. Whataya say, Jessie?"

Could it be true? Would I really be in California tomorrow? Reunited with Mama and Daddy? And traveling by airplane? A chill ran through me and tears came into my eyes. I knew at that moment Mama's prayer had finally been answered. Hazel Womack had to be my guardian angel. She even had wings—airplane wings! *Thank you, Lord!*

"Yes!" I shouted. "Oh, yes!"

"Hazel's taking me too," Tom said. "She said she can take me on to Harvest-of-Gold where I can take care of a little old business." He winked at me.

I wasn't too sure what he meant. Was he talking about digging up that gold and turning it over to the authorities? Or was he intending to split it with Lavern?

Just then, I noticed a shadow on the floor near the door. Someone stood outside the room listening. Who—

"Then it's settled," Hazel said. "Henry's made you

some of his famous potato soup. Best you'll get in all of
Arizona. You just eat up and get some more rest."

"Thank you, Mr. Womack," I said, nodding at her
brother. His entire head reddened as he smiled back. He
seemed about as shy as Hazel seemed bold.

After they left I ate my dinner. Henry's soup was the
best I'd ever eaten. Then I lay back down. Victoria
scratched around in her box. Since I had slept so long, I
remained awake, thinking of all the events of the past
week. It was truly a miracle that the Lord had brought me
this far and was about to bring me home. Home to Mama
and Daddy.

For the first time in over six months, I felt a wonderful
sense of peace.

* * *

Crash!
"Drat!"
I woke up, surprised that I'd fallen asleep and surprised
at the darkness surrounding me. What was that sound?

I sat up in bed and looked, sleepy-eyed, around the
room. I didn't see anything, but I felt something cold
pressed against my neck.

"OK, girlie, get up and get dressed," a voice came at
me in the dark. "Make it snappy and make it quiet."

Lavern! What on earth was he doing in here?

"What—?" I began, but his hand came up and covered
my mouth.

"I told you to be quiet. I've got a gun here, girlie. Now get these clothes on."

He threw my clothes at me and dropped my shoes and socks on the bed.

I shuddered with fear. Could this really be happening? But something in the man's voice and his touch showed me he meant business. I dressed in the dark room, not really seeing Lavern, but I could hear his breathing.

"Take your stuff too," he ordered. "We're gonna be taking a trip."

"A trip to where?" I whispered.

"Why, to California, girlie," he sneered. "Just where you've been aiming to be all along."

I grabbed the Bible off the wicker table. Then I squatted beside my bed.

I started to pick up Victoria to take her with me. Something made me pause. *She'd be better off here,* I told myself. *Just look at the box Henry got for her. And the worms.* I reached into the wooden crate. Victoria! I had brought her so far, protected her with every ounce of strength I could muster, and loved her.

"Oh, Victoria," I whispered. "Dear, sweet, Victoria." It was so dark in the room I couldn't see her. But I felt her warm, soft nose as she sniffed my hand. Tears came into my eyes. This was worse than saying good-bye to my doll Marjorie. It hurt almost as much as when I'd said good-bye to Mama and Daddy six months ago. I began to understand how much they must have hurt when they said good-bye to me.

"C'mon," Lavern grumbled.

I wiped my eyes and touched Victoria's ridged back. She was so small and helpless, but she was better off here with Hazel and Henry. They'd take good care of her.

Lavern yanked me to my feet. It was dark, but I imagined her looking up at me with those little black eyes. My heart tore apart.

"G-good-bye, Victoria," I sobbed, the tears trailing across my cheeks. "I'll never forget you."

"Yeah and stay off the highway," mumbled Lavern.

I spun on him and said, "You are a vile man."

"Just keep your mouth shut, girlie, or we'll be takin' that armadillo along as breakfast."

He led me downstairs in the darkness. I wanted to cry out, but I remembered Tom's words when the armed bank robbers in Gallup threatened us. "Do what they say, Jessie."

We went out to the back porch. A small light flickered, and I saw Tom asleep on a pile of blankets.

Lavern nudged Tom awake with his shoe. "C'mon, you old cuss. Get up. Get up now."

Tom was slow to rouse, but when he finally woke up, he sat up quickly.

"What in tarnation—"

"Just hush your mouth, Tennessee Tom," Lavern threatened. "You see this gun? I've got it pointed right at little girlie here. If you want to keep her safe, you'll get up, get dressed, and grab all your things. We're clearing out—now."

"Lavern, have you finally lost your mind?" Tom said.

"Probably. C'mon," was all Lavern said.

I guessed Tom figured Lavern meant business because he pulled on his green boots and grabbed his shirt and hat. But before he took another step he warned Lavern, "You harm one hair of that child's head and you'll be sorry you were ever born."

"I'm already sorry," Lavern replied. "Let's go."

In minutes we stood outside in the street. I heard Lavern jingle some keys, car keys. He planned to steal Hazel's car!

"Climb in," he ordered.

"But—"

He shoved me into the front seat. The door slammed behind me.

"Tom, you drive," Lavern said.

Tom hesitated beside the car. "They rescue you, take you in, feed you, put you up for the night, and you steal their car."

"Spare me the sermons, Tom. Just get in and drive. Remember I've got a gun pointed at this girlie."

Tom climbed behind the wheel and Lavern got into the back seat. Through the windshield I saw the stars burning in the night sky. I wanted to cry out to them, to someone. How could this be happening?

Tom started the car and it lurched away from the curb. I looked back at Hazel's great old house as we sped away.

I was being kidnapped!

Chapter 14

How could this be happening? Just a few hours ago, Hazel had told me she would fly me to San Bernardino. I'd find the McCallister farm and Mama and Daddy and everything would be right again. But now I was hostage to a deranged man hungry for loot.

I had to get out of this, but I felt weak and worn out. I hugged my Bible close and leaned against the car door. The town faded away and we rode through a dark forest. Staring straight ahead, I heard the steady *ka-chunk ka-chunk ka-chunk* of the car.

Streaks of red and yellow flamed up in the sky behind us. Dawn. Friday, May 10! Mama and Daddy would be leaving the farm by noon this very day!

The sun came up. The forest seemed to disappear with the light. Ahead, more mountains lined the horizon. Beyond them, I felt sure, lay California.

Tom cleared his throat. "Lavern, what do you say when we get near San Bernardino, we let this young lady out?"

I sat up. *Dear Lord, please let the man say "yes"!*

"Just keep driving," Lavern ordered.

"Well, why not?" Tom asked. "You got me. I've got the

map. In fact, I'll just give you the map, and you can let us both out at San Bernardino."

The map! I'd forgotten all about it. Tom didn't even know I had taken it from his boot heel. It was still tucked into the pages of my Bible.

"And how'm I supposed to read a forty-year-old home-made map?" Lavern answered. "This Harvest-of-Gold—it must of changed a lot over the years, what with buildings and such. That map's worthless to anyone but you. I need you."

"All right, but you don't need Jessie," Tom said.

Lavern laughed. "Sure, Tom. I'm not the fool you take me for. That girlie's my insurance. You'll do what you're told as long as I have this gun on her."

Lavern would never let me go. Fear gripped me. Hot tears blazed in my eyes. I was no crybaby, but I felt truly scared just then. Not just because of Lavern and his gun. I feared I'd miss Mama and Daddy. Maybe *never* find them.

I huddled in the corner of the front seat, wiping my tears on the stiff cuff of my shirt. Then I stared at the mountains, feeling numb and empty inside.

A long, long time passed. I became hungry, but Lavern made no mention of food. The sun kept rising in the sky.

The desert appeared, sudden like. Everywhere I looked I saw sand and dried brush. It reminded me of Kansas after a big blow. Nothing could grow, nothing could live. I thought, *this place looks just like what I ran away from.* I even tried to pretend I was traveling through Kansas with

Mama and Daddy, headed west. Life in California would be so much better. Daddy'd find us a farm or get a good job. There'd be no more dust storms, no more trouble with banks.

But it was no use. I could smell Lavern, and Tom didn't look anything like Daddy.

The desert wind blew hot. It swirled in through the window but brought no relief. We passed around a jar of water and a bag of biscuits, no doubt stolen from Hazel.

A longer time passed and finally the landscape changed. I saw trees, scrubby brush, and grass, then a sign:

San Bernardino
15 miles

San Bernardino! Only 15 miles! I wanted to shout for joy.

"I know what you're thinking, girlie," Lavern's harsh voice warned. "Just forget it. You ain't getting out."

I fought the urge to talk back. I didn't want Lavern riled. I had to be ready to get away.

From somewhere came a funny sound. Something like a bee buzzing, only far off. But soon it grew louder.

"We're gonna have to stop for water after crossing that desert," Tom said. "And gas pretty soon."

Lavern shuffled in the back seat. "All right, all right," he replied. "The next stop. But don't forget this gun."

A stopping place! My chance! I sat up and readied myself. Mama and Daddy were so close now.

Then that buzzing sound returned.

I looked out the window and saw only trees. The sound seemed to be coming from the sky. I glanced up. A red airplane circled above us. I wanted to watch it, but I needed to keep my eyes on the road. Be ready, I told myself.

We passed another sign. San Bernardino—only 10 miles away!

Still the plane droned on above us.

"What's that crazy pilot doing?" Lavern asked. I glanced back at him. He was staring out the back window, the gun aimed off to the side. I wondered, could I reach back and grab—?

The buzzing grew louder.

"Whoaaaa!" Lavern cried. *"Look out!"* He ducked down.

I spun back around just in time to see the wheels of the plane drop down in front of the windshield. Wow!

Tom stomped on the brakes. The plane shot up into the air.

"You crazed fool!" Lavern cried at the roof of the car. He waved the gun around like a wild man.

Tom kept driving. I looked at him. He appeared calm, even smiling. He glanced at me and mouthed a word: "Hazel."

Hazel! I rolled down my window to get a better look. The red plane circled above us again.

"What's that maniac pilot doing now?" Lavern demanded.

I ignored him and watched as the plane swung back around behind us and began another dive.

"He's coming at us again!" Lavern screamed. "Drive, Tom, *drive!*" He leaned out the window and pointed the gun at the sky.

"He's going to shoot Hazel!" I cried.

Tom slammed on the brakes again and Lavern crashed into the seat.

"Whatta you doing?" Lavern demanded. "That fool's comin' at us again! Step on it, old man!"

The drone of the airplane's engine grew louder. I looked behind us. Hazel's plane sailed out of the sky again and dropped low.

"Awwk, here it comes!" yelled Lavern.

Tom swung his fist in the air and cried, "Thatta girl!" The steering wheel jerked and the car swerved. Then it cut to the left and screeched off the road.

We bounced down a small hill, skidded across a patch of mud and rock, and headed for a row of trees! Heaven help us! Tom yanked the wheel. The car skidded sideways. I scrambled to the floor and curled into a ball like Victoria would, my Bible clutched to my chest. My heart raced as I waited for the smash. Then I heard Tom yell, "Oh, no!"

CRASH!

The car rammed into something. I jerked forward in the narrow space on the floorboard. *Ow!* Above me Tom groaned.

We rocked to a dead stop.

For a moment I couldn't catch my breath, couldn't move, but I thought, *I'm OK. I'm still alive. Thank You, Lord!*

Tom and Lavern groaned.

I crawled up into the seat. No broken bones!

Tom hunched over the wheel, holding both hands to his head. Lavern lay sprawled across the back seat. With the gun still in one hand, he felt his arms and legs as if checking to see they were still there.

The car's engine, though still running, shook and made a banging noise. Tom's side window looked like a spider-web of cracked glass.

Then I saw what we had hit—a post supporting a large sign. When I saw what was on that sign, I gasped.

Pictured was a lovely orchard of fruit trees with blue sky and pure white clouds above. In front of the trees children smiled and held up apples and pears and cherries.

The sign read:

The harvest is in and the fruit is heavenly!
McCallister Farm
Quality fruits and produce since 1924

McCallister Farm! The very place I could find Mama and Daddy. I had to be so close!

To the left lay a large field. Scattered across most of it, I saw hundreds of vehicles and tents. A narrow stretch of the field was empty. And it was on this empty field that I watched Hazel's red plane swoop out of the sky again and land.

"That crazy pilot," Lavern growled. He sat up and

waved the gun around again.

Tom still leaned against the steering wheel, holding his head. The poor man had been injured. I reached up and touched his forehead. He flinched.

"Come on," barked Lavern, "get this jalopy outta here."

When Tom didn't answer, Lavern pushed at him. Tom groaned.

"Can't you see he's hurt?" I said.

Lavern grumbled and opened his door. I looked at the plane and saw Hazel hop down. She waved her arms and yelled something. Lavern opened Tom's door.

"Move over, Tom, I'll drive," Lavern barked.

My chance to get away!

I glanced at the old man behind the wheel. We'd come so far together. He'd helped me all along, I realized. How could I leave him now, when he was hurt?

But the thought of Mama and Daddy nearby sang out to me. I said quietly, "I'm sorry, Tom. I don't want to leave you. But I've got to go."

I grabbed my Bible, opened the door, and jumped out.

"*Hey!*" Lavern called out after me. "Get back here!"

I ran for Hazel. He could try to shoot me, but I wouldn't stop. Not now, not with Mama and Daddy so close.

I ran right into the safety of Hazel's arms.

"Jessie!" she cried. "Are you all right?"

I couldn't talk. Tears flooded my eyes. Hazel squeezed me tightly.

I heard the engine of Hazel's car roar. I turned to see it bump up the hill, back to the road.

My heart ached at the sight of the car leaving. It would be the last I'd ever see of Tom. I shut my eyes and prayed silently for his safety.

Then, sighing and turning back to Hazel, I said, "How'd you find us?"

She smiled. "My car's got a big red X painted on the roof. Henry and I've had to identify it from the air before. Sure came in handy today since those varmits stole my car. I've already reported both of them to the police."

A sudden chill ran through me. "But Tom didn't steal your car. Lavern did. He took me and Tom hostages."

"I figured as much—at least about you, Jessie," Hazel said. The look in her eye made me think she regarded Tom as the same kind of varmint as Lavern.

"Tom's hurt," I told her. "He hit his head when we ran into that sign back there."

"Oh, he can take care of himself until help arrives." She pulled a watch from the pocket of her leather jacket and consulted it. "Getting on 10:30. What say I give you a short airplane ride over to where your parents are."

My parents!

"Let's get moving," she urged.

She hustled me over to her plane where a group of people had gathered. Where had they come from? Then I remembered the camp full of cars and trucks and tents.

Though I only had an hour and a half to get to the farm and find my parents, I kept thinking about poor Tom, about how he'd hurt his head and all.

A girl about my age came up to me.

"Didja ride on this aeroplane?" she asked.

I shook my head. "Do you know exactly where the McCallister farm is?"

She replied, "Sure. We was gonna work there, but they had too many folks, so we come to this here camp. The farm's just down the road a piece. Then you head right a ways. It's a bigun. Bigger'n any I ever seen."

By now more people had gathered around Hazel's plane. She turned to them and yelled out in her raspy voice, "You folks best clear away from this plane. I sure don't want anyone to get hurt."

The people moved back.

Hazel handed me a leather cap, a pair of goggles, and a bandanna. "Here, Jessie. Put these on. Tie that bandanna around your mouth and nose or you'll be spitting radiator juice for a month."

I put the cap on. It fit pretty loose. I put the goggles on, but I stopped before putting on the bandanna.

"Come on, child," Hazel urged. "Time's awastin'."

"But Tom?" I asked her. "What about him?" I searched her face for some sign that Tom would be all right.

"He'll probably get sent to jail for stealing my car," she declared.

"But I told you *Lavern's* the car thief. Tom hurt his head. He might not be able to tell the police what really happened."

I thought of Lavern's destination—Harvest-of-Gold, California. Just a few miles past San Bernardino. The place on the map where the bank loot was buried. Then I remembered the map! I flipped open my Bible and found the old map I had taken from Tom's boot heel.

"Oh, no," I said to Hazel. "I've got the map."

"The map to what, child?"

"The map to—Oh, never mind," I said. "This is just awful. Lavern'll find out Tom doesn't have the map. He may do something crazy. I...I—"

Hazel gripped me by the arms. "Jessie, we need to leave now. Are you ready or not?"

Tom. Tom. I couldn't stop thinking about him, how I needed to help him. I knew if he went to jail again at his age, it would be the end of him. He couldn't take more years behind bars. But what about Mama and Daddy? I had just enough time to get to them before they left the farm.

"Child, we need to take off—*now*," Hazel said.

Chapter 15

I looked at Hazel for the longest time. I wanted to say, "Let's go to the McCallister farm!" I wanted to be with Mama and Daddy so much it hurt. But I thought of Tom, poor gentle Tom, injured, the police after him for no reason, and Lavern about to turn on him because he wouldn't have the map. The map *I'd* taken.

I knew what I had to do.

"I want to go to Harvest-of-Gold," I said.

"Harvest-of-Gold!" she exclaimed. "Are you touched? You said you only had till noon to get to that farm."

"I do, but Tom needs me."

"But what if your folks leave?" Hazel asked.

I shook my head, not wanting to think about that. I swallowed hard and repeated, "I have to help Tom."

Hazel shook her head too. Her mouth tightened as she spoke. "I can't let you do this. You can't throw away your only chance to find your parents. I *won't* let you. Get in the plane. There's not much time left."

She was right. I *should* go to the McCallister farm. It had been my destination six days ago when I set out from Liberal. I might never have this chance again. But I just couldn't leave Tom to the police or to Lavern. I couldn't!

I took a step back. "Sorry, ma'am. I'm not going to that farm. Not now. Not with Tom in danger. If you don't take me, I'll just have to find another way."

She gazed at me like she couldn't believe what I was saying. Then she spoke in her raspy voice, "You're stubborner than I am, Jessie Land. That's mule-stubborn and not very smart. But all right. I'll take you to Harvest-of-Gold, wrong as that may be."

She helped me into the front cockpit, tugged my seatbelt snug, and patted my arm. "I'd take you as a friend any day of the week," she declared, her eyes shining.

Hazel shooed people away from the plane again. When the big propeller started up, it made a tremendous roar. I felt as if I were trapped in a barrel with a thousand bees.

Before taking off, Hazel climbed on the wing and yelled, "Watch for the red *X* on my car."

I nodded and she climbed into the other cockpit.

The plane started bumping along the ground picking up speed. We went faster and faster and I felt a rush of fear. I closed my eyes and said, *Dear Lord, keep us safe. Don't let us crash or anything. Be with Tom and protect him too. And if possible please help me find Mama and Daddy.*

Then just as I thought we were about to lift into the sky, the engine made this funny sputtering sound. We slowed down and bumped to a halt.

The engine coughed twice and died.

"Dadburned plane!" yelled Hazel. "Of all times to conk out on me."

She jumped from the cockpit.

"What's wrong?" I asked, scrambling down after her.

"Probably a clogged fuel line or something," she answered. "Sorry, Jessie, this's gonna delay us a bit."

I looked around at the grown-ups and kids staring at us. No one made a move to come closer. I felt helpless as I stood by and watched Hazel at work on the engine.

Gazing at the camp, I thought about Mama and Daddy out here in California, trying to find work, trying to scrape together enough money to make a new home, to put down new roots, to send for me.

After a while folks edged up to the plane and inspected it again. They behaved like it was a rocket ship from space, like they had never seen such a contraption before.

Fixing the plane took Hazel half an hour or so. Then we had to clear everyone away again. We got resettled in the cockpits, and Hazel started it up. The engine still sounded like a thousand bees in a barrel.

We set off down the field once more, picking up speed. This time I shut my eyes tight and said another prayer. When I looked up, the scenery blurred around me. I felt pressed back into my seat. Then, with a whoosh, we left the ground and soared up into the sky. My stomach fluttered. The biscuit I'd eaten earlier threatened to come up. I swallowed hard, forcing it to stay put.

We sailed high in the air, circling over the camp. It looked like a sea of automobiles. As far as I could see, black cars and pickups and every other kind of vehicle wedged in close to each other. Tents rose up in the narrow spaces between cars. Smoke from campfires curled up toward us. Some folks below looked up. No one waved. I sensed the misery in that camp. I hoped Mama and Daddy had never lived in a place like that.

The plane climbed higher and the camp disappeared.

My first airplane ride! I couldn't believe we were hanging in space this far above everything else. The plane vibrated and the wind blew fierce. Some brown, watery stuff splattered against the windshield and blew back onto my goggles and bandanna. The engine roared. Despite the excitement, I didn't understand the attraction for flying. A person could go stone deaf riding around in an airplane all the time.

I watched the trees and fields become desert again. We stayed up above the highway where the cars moved along resembling tiny, black bugs. A long time passed.

I watched for a car with a red *X* on the roof. When I didn't see it, worries popped into my head. Maybe Lavern turned off on some side road. Or maybe Harvest-of-Gold wasn't even on Route 66.

Some time later I spotted it. The red *X*. Plain as day. It was parked across the highway from a bright-yellow building.

I waved to Hazel, but she nodded. She'd seen it too.

The plane dropped fast. I hadn't been too nervous way up over the highway, but landing on it was something else. We swooped down. The nose dipped and it looked like we would crash. *Dear Father in heaven!* I held my breath, shut my eyes, and gripped the edge of the cockpit, waiting for the smash.

The plane jerked, then bounced. My heart bounced too, right up to my throat. I kept my eyes shut. Death comes to us all, but I saw no need to look it direct in the eye. Then I sensed the plane slowing down. The engine's roar eased up.

I opened my eyes and saw us rolling along the highway! We had made it!

Hazel pulled the plane off the road and parked it. She shut the engine down.

I tore off the goggles, the leather helmet, and the rusty-water-stained bandanna. I undid my seat belt and grabbed my Bible. Hazel helped me climb to the ground.

Where on earth were we? Where were Tom and Lavern?

Across the highway stood a row of ramshackle buildings of gray, splintered wood and sagging roofs. Beyond them I saw a gas station and beyond that a little yellow building with a sign out front.

Gus' Eat Rite Cafe and Curio Shop
Harvest-of-Gold, California

Harvest-of-Gold! Could this truly be the place where Tom had buried the stolen bank loot?

I saw no people around. Beside the café sat an old rust-eaten pickup truck. No one had even appeared to gawk at the plane.

In front of the airplane there was only a cemetery.

Beyond the cemetery four trees swayed in a warm breeze.

"Where are they?" I asked Hazel.

"I don't see 'em anywhere." She took off her helmet and threw it into the plane. "I'll run over to that café and see if the police've been here."

She bolted across the highway.

Then I heard Lavern's voice crying out, "*Liar!* You dirty liar! Hand it over!"

His voice came from the trees on the other side of the cemetery.

I raced toward the voice, dodging old headstones and wooden grave markers. Fear gripped me. Lavern had acted crazy enough just trying to get his hands on the few dollars I had. No telling what he'd do to get the loot Tom had buried.

Beyond the first tree I found them. Lavern had his gun aimed at Tom and Tom sat on the ground with his boots off, the heels pried off both of them.

Lavern swung around, pointing the gun at me. "Just hold up there, girlie," he warned. "I figured we hadn't seen the last of you."

I said, "The police are on their way. Your outlaw days are numbered, Lavern Brewster."

I edged over to Tom despite Lavern's warning. Bending down, I spied a large red bump on his forehead. But when he saw me, he winked and smiled.

I threw my arms around him. "Tom, I feared you were hurt bad."

He hugged me back. "Well, I was, missy. That mishap

back there banged me up a little. But I'm feeling better now." At once he pulled back. "Wait a minute. What time is it? You're supposed to be at that farm by noon, ain't you?"

I nodded.

He squinted up at the sun. "It's gotta be noon now—or close to it."

"I just had to know if you were all right," I told him.

"But what about your folks, Jessie? How will you ever find them if they've left that farm?"

I didn't have time to think about it. Lavern leaned closer and poked me with the gun.

"I hate to break up this tender reunion, but we're here for a purpose," he said. "Awright, Tom. Quit stallin'. Gimme that map or your little friend here—"

"Look, you selfish galoot," began Tom, "I told you the map's gone. Besides, this girl's got to get to that farm."

"The map—I want it," Lavern insisted.

I broke in. "He doesn't have it." Lavern's eyes darted angrily toward me. "I do."

I looked at Tom and explained how I'd taken the map from his boot heel the morning after the flood.

"Then give it here, girlie," Lavern butted in.

"Don't do it, Jessie," Tom said.

Lavern pointed the gun at Tom and cocked the hammer. "You'd best keep still, Tennessee Tom, or I'll bury you in the same hole you buried that loot."

I held out my Bible. The pages fell open to where my dollar was hid. Lavern spied it and snatched it up.

"So this's the precious fortune you promised me," he said. "Well, I got you here, so it's mine. Now the map."

I watched as Lavern stuffed my last dollar into his coat pocket.

Flipping through the Bible, I found the folded sheet of paper. I took it out and held it by two fingers just out of his reach.

"Give it here," Lavern demanded.

I knew I should just hand him the map, but I couldn't. I saw his fingers tighten on the gun. The gun aimed right at Tom's heart.

Chapter 16

Lavern reached for the map, but I yanked it back.

"Hand it over now!" he demanded.

I glanced at Tom and he simply shook his head.

"Gimme...." Lavern spat, grabbing at it.

I let go of the map. The wind caught it and it sailed high in the air.

"Awk!" Lavern cried. "The *map!* The *map!*"

He dropped the gun and took off after the fluttering piece of paper. The man had no wits when it came to money.

"Hurry, Tom!" I exclaimed. "Let's get out of here before he comes back."

Tom fixed his boot heels, pulled on his boots, and got up. "He ain't gonna find the loot with that map. Probably not with any map."

I searched his face. "Why?"

Tom smiled in a distant kind of way, like he was remembering back to times past. "I don't have the slightest idea where it's buried. I mean, I buried it in an open field just outside town. But it looks like the town has come and gone since. In fact, near as I can figure"—he started laughing—"I buried it right around here. And you know how folks're always digging in a cemetery."

With Lavern still chasing the map, we hurried toward the road. Hazel had come back across the highway and was inspecting her car.

Beside a wooden grave marker I stopped and hugged Tom again. "I'm so glad you weren't hurt bad. I was worried about you when we ran off the road."

He hugged me back. I thought I saw a tear in his eye, but he reached up and rubbed his face and he looked normal again.

"Look, Jessie," he began. "Listen . . . well. . . ." His eyes dropped to the ground. "You came after me. . . . You didn't need to do that. Does that mean you forgive me?"

Forgive? I gazed at him, thinking of all he'd done to help me. I could barely remember the wrongs. "Yes, of course I forgive you."

I remembered the page in my Bible where I had made the mark beside his initials. I opened the book and flipped to the back. My eyes first settled on the page with *M&D* with two marks. *I forgive you too, Mama and Daddy.* Then the page with all the marks under *AE. Forgive Aunt Edna? Could I ever do that?* I looked at the single mark beneath *T.* It had been foolish to keep this list. And wrong.

"What's that you got there, missy?" Tom asked.

I tore out the marked pages and handed Tom the Bible. Then I tore the pages into tiny pieces. I tossed them into the air and they scattered, blowing across the cemetery, some catching on the grave markers.

"It wasn't anything," I told him. I looked carefully at him and said, "Tom, there's something I never told you."

"It don't matter, Jessie."

"But it does," I said. "Remember when you asked me in Liberal why I stayed behind and my parents went on to California?"

He nodded.

Looking at the scattered pieces of paper, I said, "Well, I...I didn't tell you the whole truth. They didn't leave me because it'd be easier without a child along. The truth is my...my aunt gave them money for the trip. I got left behind to work off the loan. It was the only way they could go. It's just that I felt like I'd been *sold* and for the longest time I couldn't forgive them. It seemed so...so *shame*ful."

Tom wrapped his arms around me and hugged me, blotting my tears with his shirt. "You know, it don't seem so shameful to me. Sometimes folks'll put money in something as an investment. Your folks had a heap of faith in you. They knew you'd do all right."

I smiled up at him. I knew at that moment I'd not only forgiven this man, I'd grown to love him too.

"Tom, do you think Hazel would give me a ride to that farm?" I asked. "My parents might still be somewhere around there." I wasn't sure they would be, but I still clung to the hope of finding them.

"Sure, missy," he said.

Glancing at Hazel beside her car, I said, "Well, we'd better hurry then."

Hazel not only agreed to drive us, she drove fast. I knew Mama and Daddy had probably left the farm, so I kept alert. I watched for the old, beat-up, black Essex they'd gone west in.

Everywhere I looked I saw things I'd never before seen. I saw a four-poster bed set up beside a rusty automobile and covered with dirty little kids, all asleep. I saw some folks wearing nothing but rags and no shoes, shuffling along beside the road. I saw a woman on a bicycle balancing a big pot on top of her head.

Suddenly, a police car, its siren blasting, zoomed down the highway, headed for Harvest-of-Gold. Lavern! In spite of the way he'd treated me, I hoped they'd go easy on him.

Then we passed a white car pulled off the highway. A woman with red hair stood beside a man looking at something spread across the hood.

There was something about that red hair, all swept up on top of her head.

"Stop!" I cried, surprising Hazel.

She braked and we skidded to a halt.

"What is it, Jessie?" Tom asked, just as surprised.

Spinning around to look out the back window, I said, "That lady. She looks—" Then I got a better look at the man beside her.

Daddy!

I yanked at the door handle and threw myself out of the car. *"Daddy!"* I screamed.

I ran toward the white car. My heart thundered in my chest.

"Daddy!" I cried once more, gasping for air.

This time he heard me. He looked up. Standing beside him, Alice Townes shielded her eyes and glanced around too. Then one of the car's doors swung open. Another red-headed woman appeared.

Mama!

I felt like I was in one of those dreams where you need to run but can't move fast enough—where you want to cry out but your voice won't work.

Finally, I managed to yell, *"Mama! Daddy!"*

Mama's hands flew to her mouth. Daddy ran to meet me. I fell into his arms.

"Oh, Daddy, Daddy," I cried.

"Jess, sweetheart, I—I—" I felt his tears against my cheek.

Mama ran to us. We all stood hugging and crying.

Mama touched my hair and sobbed, "My land! It's just like the picture in the paper."

I didn't know what she meant by "the picture in the paper," but I told her how Aunt Edna hadn't wanted to be bothered with my hair and how she cut it all off.

"Edna!" Mama exclaimed. "Why, I'll give her a piece of my mind."

I hugged her and said, "No, Mama, it's all right. We're together now. That's what's important."

Alice Townes came up and I hugged her. Then she said, "When I got back to Los Angeles, the paper ran your picture. The one I took at that gas station. And your parents saw it."

"We'd already left that farm, honey," Daddy explained. "The work hadn't lasted long. I was looking for a job, so I bought a newspaper and we saw your picture. We called the paper and they let us talk to Miss Townes."

"All I remembered was the name of that town you mentioned," Alice Townes said. "Harvest-of-Gold."

"We've been looking for you, honey," Mama added, "but the town wasn't on the map."

I remembered Tom. I pulled myself away from Mama and Daddy. "I want you to meet someone," I said, drawing them by the hands.

Tom stood a short distance off watching the three of us. Shy like.

"Mama, Daddy," I said, "meet Tom McCauley. He brought me here. Mama, he was the guardian angel you prayed for."

Tom's pale face reddened. Daddy shook hands with him and said, "Thank you, sir, for taking care of my little girl."

"Was a privilege," Tom replied. "I never knew anyone quite like her. She's got gumption."

Hazel joined us and I introduced her too. She seemed restless, as if she wanted to be on her way.

"I think I'll go back and get the Waco," she declared. "Go look up a friend in Los Angeles who makes moving pictures. Collects Indian art too. Maybe you've heard of him. Name's Will Rogers."

"*Will Rogers!*" I exclaimed.

Tom brightened. "Mind if I go with you? I'd kinda like to see one of these motion picture outfits. Maybe they have a need for some old coot like me who knows the truth about the Wild West."

"Let's go!" Hazel replied.

We hugged and cried some more. Then Tom and Hazel took off in Hazel's car.

When the car was a tiny, black spot, I turned away and wiped the tears from my eyes. I stared at the road going the other direction. Stretching all the way from Liberal to here. It had been a long way home.

I smiled to myself when I thought of Tom meeting up with Will Rogers and telling all the moving picture folks about the real West. I could see him doing that. Decked out in black, his eyes sharp and green boots polished, he'd notice every little detail, just like he did that time we went to the moving picture show. He'd surprise them all. Tennessee Tom was a man like no other.

And the best guardian angel I had ever met.

ABOUT THE AUTHOR

Jerry Jerman lives in Norman, Oklahoma with his wife Charlene, twin daughters Emily and Hadley, son Andrew, and two cats. He likes Mexican food, baseball, traveling throughout the American Southwest, and really fast roller coasters. When he's not writing about the journeys of Jessie Land, he keeps busy with church and family activities. Now and then he does something crazy like late October sailboat racing in a "frostbite regatta."